Nurse Stuck in the Snow

ANNETTE WETHERLY

Trafford
PUBLISHING®

Order this book online at www.trafford.com
or email orders@trafford.com

Most Trafford titles are also available at major online book retailers.

Design and photography by Annette Wetherly.

Note for Librarians: A cataloguing record for this book is available from Library
and Archives Canada at www.collectionscanada.ca/amicus/index-e.html

Printed in Victoria, BC, Canada.

ISBN: 978-1-4251-7632-7

*Our mission is to efficiently provide the world's finest, most comprehensive
book publishing service, enabling every author to experience success.
To find out how to publish your book, your way, and have it available
worldwide, visit us online at www.trafford.com*

Trafford rev. 8/5/2009

Trafford
PUBLISHING®   www.trafford.com

North America & international
toll-free: 1 888 232 4444 (USA & Canada)
phone: 250 383 6864 ♦ fax: 812 355 4082

To all who love adventure and the challenges it brings.

Contents

Photographs

Chapter 1

ℭ

MY FIRST ARCTIC COMMUNITIES - CAMBRIDGE BAY AND PELLY BAY

I GRADUATED IN 1989, from the University of Victoria with a BSN degree. After practicing nursing and working in Victoria for the past 13 years with the developmentally challenged I really wanted to escape my present life style and find a new road through life. It was time for a new experience.

Due to a nurses' strike no work was available in British Columbia. I decided to flex my heels and off I went to try an out-post nursing job in the North West Territories. Just as I was about to leave, I received an invitation to join my old school colleagues from the Convent of the Sacred Heart in Rome. We had been invited to the canonization of the founder of our school, Saint Madeline Sophie, and would have a private audience with Pope John Paul II. I was sorry I was unable to go to this once in a lifetime celebration. I had also decided not to attend my convocation at University of Victoria.

In May 1989, I landed in Yellowknife, the capital of NWT 24 hour daylight, snow and seven feet of ice on the ocean, not exactly what we in the south think of as summer. How was I going to adjust to this new experience? I met four other nurses who were of the same mind set as myself. Pat was from Nova Scotia, Charlene and Maureen from Alberta, Carol from New Zealand and myself from Victoria.

The next day, we spent time at Stanton hospital meeting staff, learning X-ray and laboratory techniques. In the evening, I met up with the executive secretary to the North West Territories' Legislative Assembly whom I had met in 1986 on a Holland America cruise to South America and Caribbean on board SS Rotterdam.

Next day the nurses met with the Health Department and I encountered Kate who had also done her midwifery in Aberdeen. We received our Hepatitis B shot and had to take more vaccine with us to give ourselves the next two doses of the series. The following morning we left for the Kitikmoet Health Board head quarters in Cambridge Bay. Health in the Arctic is divided into five administrative regions: the McKenzie Area whose headquarters is in Yellowknife; Inuvik area whose headquarters is in Inuvik; Keweetin whose headquarters is in Rankin Inlet; Kitikmoet whose headquarters is in Cambridge Bay and the Baffin area whose headquarters is in Iqaluit. The latter four regions are beyond the tree line.

The NWT Air plane landed on the airstrip in Cambridge Bay, Victoria Island. Little did I know that I was going to land and take off from there many more times in the next six years. The welcoming party was waiting: Jimmy, the janitor, from the Health Centre greeted me with "*Solomon Bar*" which doesn't really mean anything and over time Jimmy and I would greet each other this way. Also welcoming us Susan, Nurse in Charge at the Health Centre, who to this day is one of my long standing friends and Robin, the Regional Nursing Officer, Iona Maksagak, the Community Health Representative and her mother, Helen, the Commissioner for the North West Territories. Iona and I were to become very close friends over the next few years. What a warm welcome in this frozen Northern country. We drove in the Nursing Station truck to the residence and as we entered the door, Carol who had been North before, lifted the lid of a green box and said "make sure that you have enough water for your tea and teeth for the morning". I did not know why she told us this, but later discovered the reason. Permafrost is an ever-present feature in this Northern clime, which makes it impossible to put plumbing pipes underground. Water is trucked to each house or *"igloo"*, and sewage is trucked away in the same manner. The sewage is dumped on to the land at one side of the settlement resulting in a picture of verdant green in the summer months. At the other side of the hamlet is the water supply. The Inuit like to collect ice for making tea and do not use the water supply for this purpose. Brian, the doctor for the Kitikmoet Health Board warned us that we should never call for water on a Sunday as we might get the sewage truck instead. This he had learned from experience.

The following morning with teeth cleaned and a good cup of coffee, we made our way to the Health Board office to meet the staff, receive a certificate for crossing the 60th parallel and an orientation program.

Part of the orientation programme was crash survival on the Arctic Tundra and included how to find the ELT (emergency locator transmitter) how to trap Arctic hare and light a fire from the survival kit on the plane. In 1972, there had been a crash on the tundra where the medivac nurse and patients from Taloyoak (Spence Bay) had crashed on the tundra. The pilot, Martin Hartwell had not wished to fly due to poor weather conditions but the nurse insisted. The Inuit woman who was pregnant and the nurse both died on impact. Martin and an Inuit teenager with suspected appendicitis survived. Martin had two broken legs and survived by eating the nurse but the Inuit boy later died as he refused to eat the nurse, Judy Hill. Martin was stranded for 32 days and to this day Judy Hill's skis are still in the Health Centre in Taloyoak (Spence Bay). Later in the day at the Health Centre, nursing station, we met Eva, the clerk/interpreter, little Eva, the housekeeper, Valerie and Rachel two other community health Nurses, who are now both Medical Doctors.

Cambridge Bay has two Grocery stores the Co-op and the Northern; a Hunters and Trappers association store, an Anglican Church and a small recreation center with a swimming pool. The church service integrates both Inuit cultural beliefs and language with the dominant Anglican beliefs. During my week in Cambridge Bay Carol started the long process of making a sweater for me from a musk ox hide, we had purchased from the Hunters' and Trappers store. Carol and I carried the hide back to the nursing station residence and hung it out to dry off. The next task was to comb out the soft under coat, kiviat, spinning it and dyeing the wool with local flower dyes. Luckily, I escaped the combing and the following procedures, as I had to leave for my next settlement.

It was time to go to my next hamlet settlement, Pelly Bay. Jimmy took me to the airstrip along with Pat and Charlene who were both going to Gjoa Haven and Valerie who was taking a charter to Bay Chimo. Bay Chimo is a community of 20 Inuit people, one water tap and a generator for electricity. There is a lay dispenser and communications with nurses in Cambridge Bay is by radiophone. The whole world hears the conversation. Valerie's pilot was Willy Laserich, a well-known legend in the North. There had been a power outage in Pelly Bay and an electrical crew and equipment had priority on boarding the scheduled flight that Pat, Charlene and I were booked on. All the passengers were able to board but with only one item of baggage each. Big decision time so I chose my most important item which was my food. This left my two suitcases behind and they would be sent in three days time on the next scheduled flight. The first stop was Gjoa Haven where Pat and Charlene got off. We said farewell and they left the airport in a taxi for the Gjoa Haven Health Centre. While the plane was refueling and the passengers were waiting to re-board, whom did I spy on the runway but Willy with my red suitcase in hand. He said I couldn't have the nurse going to Pelly Bay without any change of clothes. Now there is room on the plane for my suitcase, my son, René, will have your other suitcase at the nursing station in Pelly Bay by noon tomorrow. Willy had been flying Valerie to Bay Chimo in the other direction from our scheduled flight so after leaving Valerie in Bay Chimo, he had followed our flight to ensure that I had a change of clothes. One only finds such kindness shown in the North.

In April 1990 the Northwest Territories Registered Nurses' Association Newsletter published this article, which describes some of these adventures. It was over the past 47 years, Laserich has made the equivalent of 800 trips around the world with a perfect safety record. Based in Cambridge Bay, N.W.T., 285 kilometres above the Arctic Circle, he has rescued stranded hunters, injured trappers and downed pilots. His winged workhorses have hauled caribou, whale meat and blubber, carried corpses to funerals, and transported hunting parties with sleds and dog teams that howled behind the pilot's seat. Flying in some of the planet's harshest conditions, his engines have iced up and shut down in mid-air forcing him to control a plunge from 2,000 metres and glide to a landing on a frozen river. He has dug his plane out of axle-deep muck and survived winter nights after emergency landings left him stranded on the tundra. Often flying when no one else would take to the air, Laserich has many tales to tell. It was February 25, 1985 Willy Laserich was sitting behind the controls of his King Aircraft, he turned to look into the back of his plane. On a stretcher lay a woman with a knife protruding from her chest that couldn't be removed until she reached the hospital for fear she would bleed to death.

On another stretcher, a woman moaned with pain from a swollen appendix. Beside a man with a serious eye injury sat the "medivac," nurse, cradling a baby who wheezed with bronchial pneumonia. Laserich gritted his teeth. This is a nightmare, he thought as icy winds of 60 kilometres an hour buffeted the plane, and the swirling snow reduced visibility to 45 metres. "We do the checklist twice," he told his son René, who was his co-pilot that day. "Nothing goes wrong that we could have prevented, *ja?*"

Laserich was taking off from the airstrip in Spence Bay, N.W.T. (now called Taloyoak and part of Nunavut). He knew that the lives of the four patients depended on his flying skills. He revved the engines and headed blindly into the elements, struggling to follow the only reference point he could see, the grooves left on the runway by the snow grader. Moments later, the plane broke through the storm into sunshine. "It was a risk, but a calculated one," is how the veteran pilot now sums up his most horrific medevac. Having landed at Spence Bay earlier that morning, he knew that 30 metres above the ground, the sky was clear, although there were still strong winds. Getting off the ground in the whiteout was tricky, but Laserich was highly experienced and knew the airstrip well. "There is bad weather, and there is dangerous weather," he says, "and in the North, it's critical that you know the difference between the two". The conditions that day were bad; had they been dangerous, he would not have flown.

I arrived in Pelly Bay; Mike and Annette Hart manage the co-op, the local grocery store that sells Inuit carvings. The Harts run the only vehicle except for skidoos and all terrain vehicles. There are no roads in Pelly Bay. Mike doubles as the Coroner and is from Winnipeg, he was also driving the taxi. There were two other passengers in the communal taxi, two young Inuit men who asked if I was the new nurse and where did I come from? I answered *yes* and *I come from Aberdeen in Scotland.* "Oh our father is from Peterhead". Peterhead is a fishing community 23 miles north of Aberdeen. In the last century many whalers came to Pelly Bay from North East Scotland and you can still hear the old Scottish tunes in the music that the Inuit play. These two men were the sons of Alex Buchan and Ernie Lyall. Ernie Lyall came north in the days of the whalers and settled in Spence Bay on the Booth Peninsula. Taloyoak is another place I will visit later in time. Alex Buchan is married to Annie, an Inuit lady who would be my Clerk interpreter in Taloyoak and Annie is also the Justice of the Peace. Alex managed the Hudson Bay store or as it is now called the Northern Store. It only took a few minutes from the airstrip to reach the health center, which overlooks the Hamlet of Pelly Bay. Cora, the Nurse in Charge greeted me and introduced me to the health centre staff: Katherine, the clerk interpreter, Theresa the housekeeper and the janitor, Gaeton who was the son of a shaman and some in the community feared this relationship. Gaeton remembers when he was a child living in the igloo on the land. When his father would dance the whole igloo shook. I was yet to meet Gabriel who was out on training preparing to be the community health representative. These five people were to set me on a course of one of my life's most rewarding adventures.

Next day true to Willy Laserich's word his son René was on the doorstep of the Nursing station at lunchtime with my blue suitcase.

The work was varied and challenging. We held weekly well baby clinics, pre and postnatal clinics with the occasional delivery and a weekly chronic disease clinic. Sick clinics are held Monday to Friday in the afternoon. School health; sexually transmitted disease tracing; home visiting the elders; accidents; laboratory and x-rays are all part of the routine. The Doctor located 800 air miles away was available for telephone consult and a monthly visit to the community. Anything that could not wait for the planned monthly visit would require medivacing to Stanton Hospital in Yellowknife or a more serious case would have to go to Edmonton. This plan only worked if the weather permitted and the medivac plane was not out on another call.

A medivac to and from Yellowknife was 4,000 air miles. If the weather was down and the satellite, which is the telephone link is out you were left to cope. The flight to Edmonton was twice the distance. If one called for a medivac especially at night one had to inform the airstrip person to see what the weather was doing and if favourable, he would prepare the runway by plowing the snow and ice and setting up the landing lights. Once the plane had landed, notify the fuel person to refuel the plane once it had landed. Today the pilot can activate the lights from the plane but nothing else has changed. The regional dentist and medical specialists visit the community at least yearly and the community health nurse keeps a ledger with referrals. Sometimes the nurse will make direct referrals to a specialist and does not always have to go through the regional doctor. The obstetrician, Pierre Lassard, visits the community twice yearly and brings a portable ultra sound machine.

During the working day Gaeton, the janitor, was responsible for taking and developing x-rays but after hours this was the nurses' job. One would look at the X ray film and attempt to make a judgment on diagnosis and treatment. The x ray was then sent out to Stanton Hospital to the radiographer for interpretation.

After hours the community members would bring a relative for translation but during clinic hours that was Katherine's job. Women were sent to Yellowknife to have their babies at 38 weeks gestation and Katherine made these travel arrangements. In later years, I was to be part of the planning process for traditional midwifery services in Northern communities.

The Hamlet of Pelly Bay is built in two concentric circles and was first settled in the early 1950's. Prior to this settlement, the Inuit people had lived in icehouses on the land. We know these as igloos, which is the word in Inuktitut for house. In the summer the community lived on the land in tents and still make this a habit today. Much earlier in the century, the Oblate fathers built the old stone church and a house for the priest down at the mouth of the River. Above the old stone church and priest's house is the old graveyard. The graveyard houses many infants and young children who died in a measles epidemic. White settlers first introduced measles and tuberculosis to the Inuit and as the Inuit had no resistance to such infectious diseases and many people succumbed to them. Pelly Bay is a community of 250 Inuit and persons over 40 years of age do not speak English but Inuktitut. Children under ten usually do not vocalize very much but answer your questions by raising their eye brows for "yes" and squinting their noses for "no". This habit continues through out the lifespan as older people accompany their speech with facial gesticulations. There is no road or sea link unless one is able to travel by small boat in the summer or dog team and skidoo in the winter. Air is the only link to the rest of the world. Hence, the Inuit culture and traditions are very much intact and food is extremely expensive. Unless it grows there everything has to be flown in and this includes anything wooden as we are beyond the tree line. Milk comes in a can or powdered and potatoes and eggs are also powdered. Fresh fruit and vegetables are very limited and expensive with a can of frozen orange juice costing three times as much in Pelly Bay as in the south of Canada. Weight is an extra cost due to freight charges. Very often there is no bread and one just has to eat pilot biscuits. The new church is in the centre of the two concentric circles and is the focal point of attention.

Pelly Bay is a strongly Catholic community and besides Father Joseph, a Belgian priest, there are two lay catechists, Bartholme and his wife Sidone. This couple had been to Rome and met the Pope. Services are conducted in Inuktitut. Each week Father Joseph would deliver a French baguette, which he had baked to every igloo in the hamlet. This is a very apt task for a man of the cloth.

Hunting and fishing are still the main occupations of this traditional community and those who cannot participate in these activities are given a part of the harvest. At the mouth of the river is a large marker, inukshuk, in the shape of a human and built of large rocks used very much as we would use a lighthouse on the ocean and one can tell exactly where one is located on the vast expanse of white frozen land. Arctic char are caught in the river either by netting or spearing. I am told that speared fish tastes better than netted fish as the adrenaline is not coursing through the fish when they are caught. Arctic char have no scales and have a more delicate flavour than salmon. Caribou are hunted, along with seal. The skins are used to make clothing and rugs that help keep one warm in a traditional igloo, out on the land and on a skidoo or dog team. Polar bear also frequent this region, as Pelly Bay is on the route that the polar bear follow each year. People in Pelly Bay fear the polar bear as these animals are the most ferocious of all the bear family. An elder told me that many years ago he had come out of his igloo only to be faced by a bear and the only way he was still alive to tell the tale was that he played dead. He had a large scar on his neck adjacent to his carotid artery, which the priest had stitched for him and saved his life. This was long before there were nurses in this area. The community health representative, Gabriel told me how he and a girl friend had hidden in a hut from a polar bear, which stalked them for over 12 hours.

Above the health centre stands the school where students attend from grades 1- 6 in Pelly Bay. Grades 7-10 go to Cambridge Bay and grades 11-12 go to Yellowknife. Next to the school is the Hamlet Council office. The Mayor heads the Hamlet Council. Meetings are conducted in Inuktitut, as are all meetings in this community and all meetings start with a prayer. I had the pleasure of accepting an invitation to attend a number of those council meetings, which were simultaneously translated for me by John Ningark who was later to become the local member of the territory's legislative assembly. Another interesting meeting that I was invited to attend was the Health Committee Meeting which the incumbent nurse was permitted to attend on invitation only. This time Celine Ningark, John's wife and local school secretary, performed the simultaneous translations. Most of the 30 –40 year old population of Pelly Bay had been sent to school in Yellowknife and were forced to speak English, learn French and study Latin by the Oblate Fathers and Sisters.

At the other end of the Hamlet is the Co-Op store. It is always wise for the community health nurse to be familiar with the stock that the store carries as it is pertinent for giving health advise. There is no point in telling someone to eat salad if the food material to make it is unavailable. One has to adjust ones thinking as to what is available in the area and the dietary customs of the population.

The Hunters and Trappers association is next to the Co-Op and next to that is the local craft shop. Dog teams surround the perimeter of the community and are tied up with four-foot chains. They are usually fed once every 3 days and do not have water. These animals are working dogs and are not treated as pets. One does not pet the dogs. This was a very hard concept for me to adjust to. When one is out and about the people greet you with a very warm handshake.

At one point alcohol was consumed in Pelly Bay but following a murder of an Inuit woman and encounters with the men from the DEW Line, Early Warning System, the Mayor and Hamlet Council had a bylaw passed to make Pelly Bay a dry town. This has had a tremendously positive influence on the community at large.

On the weekend Cora was very instrumental in educating me in the lie of the land. Standing on a high spot and looking down on an area three rings of stone are visible. These are the old campsites. The top one is where the family slept and the stone circle held down the tent so that it was not blown away in a wind. Below this is the area was where the fire was made and bones may have been boiled to feed a baby and of course water was boiled to make tea. No, not the tea we know but Labrador tea, which was made from the leaves of the Labrador plant. Food was prepared in the bottom circle. Inuit do not cook their meat or fish but cut it very finely with an ooloo knife, which has a bone handle and a curved blade. The food preparation area is rich in nitrogen and as a result moss and flowers grow profusely. Cora pointed out an old grave with a skeleton in it. This grave was built like a cairn known in this area as a cache from the French word to hide. There was only one left in the area and the skeletal remains were facing right, in a foetal position. This is the same style of burial arrangement that was used by the Stone Age people in north east of Scotland prior to the advent of Christianity. Women were facing right, and men left, both in the foetal position. In the Arctic, the coming of Christianity also ended this form of burial. In the summer, June until August, the graves are usually dug in preparation for an event and the hole is covered over with a board. In some communities this is not the custom, as superstition does not permit the digging of pre-prepared graves and therefore if a person dies in the winter, burial will not take place until the grave may be dug. The gravesite is marked with a wooden cross and earthly belongings decorate the crosses. Sometimes it is a plastic flower, a packet of cigarettes, coin money or a rosary. When snow and ice finally leave the area, usually mid June the first thing to sprout is the willow, but unlike the willow in the south, it is a low creeping bush with the usual familiar pussy willow catkins. There are no trees in this area and the wind certainly helps keep every thing close to the ground. The next plant to spring up all over the place is the tiny purple Saxifrage; one would swear that these flowers were on a time clock and so they are. 24-hour daylight May until the end of August and the entire life cycle of a plant has to operate in this time period. The scene is similar to the purple carpet created by the heather when it covers the mountains in the highlands of Scotland in August. Next to flower are the Moss Campion, the Arctic Poppy; Arctic Cotton; Mountain Avens the floral emblem of the territory; Labrador tea; Woolly Lousewort; Arctic Bell Heather; Mountain Paintbrush and Buttercups. A book of Arctic flowers compiled by Cora is held in the archives in Ottawa.

In July Cora went out on leave it was my turn to show Julie, a new nurse around. Julie had never been North before and we had fun exploring the community. One day we went for a walk on the tundra, a man came running towards us and was shouting something. As he came nearer we could hear what he was shouting, "come back you white bitches"! Not so thought I, who was this person? As he came closer, I recognized him; it was John Ningark. He asked us to come back to his summer camp where his wife and daughters were preparing a caribou carcass for drying and using an ooloo knife. Once the meat was cut into fine strips it was hung to dry in the sun on the fishing nets. We were offered a taste of the raw meat but we politely declined. All over the hamlet, lines hung between the houses, to dry arctic char, just as we might hang washing out to dry. This was the old method of preserving food when it was plentiful in the summer months and before the days of refrigeration. Once the weather had turned cold, another way to hide the meat and fish from the polar bear was in caches.

The summer games celebration was on 21 May, Victoria Day. Everyone was down on the oceanfront in the snow and the ocean had still seven feet of ice.

Skidoo and dog team races were in full swing and tea boiled on Coleman stoves. I was offered some tea, hot bannock and an ooloo sliced piece of raw caribou and seal. I gladly accepted the warm tea and bannock and thanked the person.

By the end of August the ice was beginning to form on the puddles and the days were getting shorter which meant summer was fast drawing to a close. Some people were still living in tents.

The polar bear were on the move and much to the horror of the campers a bear came to sniff out the seal caches. Next I heard that two notable hunters had shot the bear and the spoils were divided amongst the community. It was September and time for me to leave this tiny Central Eastern Arctic Community.

I walked towards the air strip and on my way there an older man took my suit case from me and carried it on his head. He did not speak English but his gesture was enough. I shook his hand and said "Koana". Gaeton, his nephew, arrived at the airstrip. I asked him to convey my thanks to his uncle for his kind gesture in helping me with my luggage. Most of the community came to the airstrip to bid me farewell. What a warm feeling this left me with and I was sad to go but I had a position waiting for me in Bella Bella on the west coast of British Columbia. As we stopped to refuel in Cambridge Bay, Carol came to the airstrip with the musk ox sweater she had knitted. It was beautifully soft and warm. The colours were dark brown, lighter brown and pinkish purple from the purple Saxifrage that covers the tundra in the spring. What a delightful surprise.

Chapter 2

໌

WAGLISLA AND THE THOMAS CROSBY V

IN SEPTEMBER 1989, I started work in the R. W. Large United Church hospital in Bella Bella or in Heiltsuk language, Waglisla, an 18-bed hospital with an emergency department and an operating theatre. Attached to the hospital is a three doctor medical clinic, a pharmacy and a laboratory. At the entrance to the hospital is an engraved plaque with the following inscription: "Mother Earth is precious and sacred. She is the dust and ashes of all our ancestors. It is through her that we become who we are. As you go forth remember your past. Live a life that touches others and remember: a gift that is given in kindness and caring will last into eternity". Written by, Arthur Vickers, Artist, a member of the Heiltsuk from Waglisla and Tshimshan from Kitkatla First Nations heritages.

Waglisla is a First Nation reserve of approximately 1500 Heiltsuk people consisting of two stores, two churches one United and one Pentecostal, a boat yard, a post office and a weekly fly in, weather permitting, from the Canadian Imperial Bank of Commerce from Port Hardy. Fishing is the main industry. This location was a far cry from the community of Pelly Bay.

I had a beachfront house next door to the hospital and the salmon almost leapt on to one's doorstep. The hospital had a fabulous Heiltsuk cook, Mrs. Humschit, and therefore one did not have to do any cooking.

The maintenance man, Mitch was a great scuba diver and would catch abalone, which we really enjoyed for a short while, until a ban on harvesting abalone was imposed. One day there were 30 sea eagles on the tree out side the hospital. Mitch explained that one could always tell where the fish were, as that is where the eagles perched waiting to dive down and catch a salmon. The minister of the United Church was Ernie Willie who was the boy in the story, by Margaret Craven "I heard the Owl call my Name".

The director of Nursing was Deanna Lawson, a lovely person who was married to a Heilsuk artist and teacher at the local school. Don Watts a fatherly figurehead was one of the doctors and he had just retired as the administrator of the three west coast cottage hospitals operated by the United Church in Bella Coola, Hazelton and Waglisla. Don had taken a refresher course and wanted to do more clinical practice. Jane Clelland, another of the three doctors and I became very friendly. The head doctor was Ivor Flemming and we had some exciting collaborative work ahead of us. I was kept busy with work and exploring the local Community and near by islands. One day I was on my days off when Jane asked me if I would like to go to the outreach clinics in Klemtu and Ocean Falls to help her see patients and act in my role as a nurse practitioner. So off we went to the floatplane dock and Ocean Falls, which used to be a thriving community when the hydro plant and forestry industry were in full swing. Today, Ocean Falls has a very small population. There are more cats than people. The cats occupy the church and sleep in the pews. The rainfall in Ocean Falls is one of the highest on the west coast rain forest area of British Columbia. There is still an hotel but few visitors and a one-room school. We spent the day doing clinics and after lunch I did some immunizations in the hotel. The children received ice cream following the immunizations. Next clinic was the following day in Klemtu, which is the home of the Kitasoo Nation. We boarded the floatplane and landed on the dock in Klemtu where Francis Robinson, an elder in the community of 1000 First Nations People, met us. Percy Star was the Chief at the time and his daughter, Marg, was the clinic clerk. I had previously met Marg when her mother had been a patient in the hospital in Waglisla. Bruce Robinson was the Community Health Representative. Another person I had met in the hospital was a young woman who was an insulin dependant diabetic and we helped her reduce her body weight so that she could come off insulin and utilize dietary and oral medication to control her blood sugar levels. Most of the family names in Klemtu were Robinson. Later in my career I was to visit Klemtu several times. It was a busy clinic and we left around 4 PM.

One evening as I was finishing my four-day rotation at the end of a twelve-hour shift, the minister from the United Church Coastal Mission Ship, Thomas Crosby V, Paul Davies, 45 from Williams Lake arrived at the hospital I thought he had come to visit the elders, but I was wrong. After taking him to meet an elder, I asked who was the next person he wished to visit. "Well I have really come to see you as I have been asked by the coast guard to have a nurse visit a pregnant lady on one of the lighthouses". I was quite taken aback and said that I had three days off but he said I would need five for the trip. So I called Deanna who agreed to cover two shifts for me. Next day, Ivor armed me with all my necessary equipment and I left for the dock to board the 80-foot vessel, Thomas Crosby V. Jane came to see me off along with Don Watt. The skipper, Mark Stevens aged 45 who read me the 16th century guidelines for food rations aboard the Crosby. The engineer, Harald Wenschuh, aged 25 from Germany via Newfoundland. Jackie, 23 was the cook and Doug, deck hand, 70. I was shown to my cabin, Don and Jane left and we cast off. Oddly enough, Paul knew Mary, a girl that I had met while studying statistics at the University of Victoria. Mary had grown up in Peterhead where her father had been the minister at the Prison there. I was in for a very different experience. In fact, the crew teased me to death. The Salon had a sign *No talking permitted* and I received a new name, "Nurse bag-pipes". Most of my time on board was spent on the bridge and despite all the ragging; we all became the firmest of friends. The dolphins would play alongside the boat, as well as nosing the bow, then dart away again only to repeat this maneuver over and over again. Harald and I became good friends and decided it was time for me to have some fun. So when we docked in Port Hardy he took me off to the pub and Paul frowned on this activity.

After a pub visit in Port Hardy, we set off for Egg Island lighthouse to see the pregnant lady and as it turned out, all was well there. In order to reach the lighthouse it was necessary to go in the Zodiac operated by Harald. This was fun except for gearing up in very heavy water safety suits. Our next stop was Bella Coola to drop off Doreen who was a Licensed Practical Nurse at the hospital in Bella Coola. This is where Sir Alexander MacKenzie carved his name on a rock when he was exploring Canada. Sir Alexander MacKenzie was from Fortrose on the Black Isle in Northern Scotland. I visited the United Church Hospital with Doreen and then her home in the Native part of the Nuxalk Village of Bella Coola. This is a fairly divided community and even the Church Services are divided. The Scandinavian Settlers' service is in the morning and the Nuxalk First Nations Service is held in the evening. Back on board the Crosby, we had invited the minister from the Church for a luncheon.

We next docked at Owikeno, a small Helsuik Village near Rivers Inlet. It was low tide and easy to walk up the ramp to shore. The community health representative met us and I went with him to do some clinical work. Although many grizzly bears had been spotted in the community I did not see any. With all my clinical work and a few elder home visits concluded we had several hours drive back to the ship. By which time, the tide had turned and the ramp was perpendicular. I proceeded to make quite the spectacle of myself. Lying at the top of the ramp with my knees bent, feet and hands flat to the floor of the ramp, I walked my way down to the deck. This was my shipmates' entertainment for the day and I was greeted by a resounding encore.

Unfortunately, my five days adventure was up and I had to return to my work in the hospital in Bella Bella. The crew requested that I make another trip of a longer duration and so I would leave Bella Bella again on the Crosby in November.

Back in Bella Bella, I attended a community wedding with 15 bridesmaids and groomsmen. The whole community attended the event, which is the custom in west coast native communities. What a feast followed, salmon galore, oolican, herring eggs, bannock and more.

The next social event was at the school and once again the whole village attended. This was a traditional celebration put on in honour of inter change non-Native students from Ontario. The Ontario students had learned and participated in traditional dances from the Queen Charlotte Islands. They had used the traditional methods to make a canoe and had made a drum and played it in the traditional fashion. The audience were given a running explanation of what was happening, which made it a most enlightening experience.

On Sundays we frequently took the water taxi over to Shearwater for a traditional Sunday roast dinner at the lodge there. Shearwater was an island that had been used by the Canadian Navy in the Second World War as a repair yard for the fleet.

On my days off, I was becoming bored so volunteered to drive in the ambulance. One day a lady from Klemtu was coming in to Waglisla by floatplane. She was in premature labour. Off we went to the floatplane dock to meet the plane. I was at the head of the stretcher going up the ramp, I felt a jolt and as I turned round, I saw that the ambulance fellow was on his knees on the dock ramp. He was wearing cowboy boots and had slipped on the wet ramp. The floatplane pilot rushed to the rescue and took hold of the foot of the stretcher and the man with the cowboy boots joined me at the top. All was well in the long run, but a lesson was learned. Do not wear cowboy boots on a wet slippery dock! The patient on the stretcher had missed a dunking in the brink. It might have been an early baptism.

Now it was time to say good-bye to Jane who was going to work in Masset on the Queen Charlotte Islands and I was off on my next trip to Port Simpson on the Thomas Crosby V. I would return to Port Simpson later in my career. Duly signed on board and given my historical 16th century maritime regulation spiel about rations allowed per person on board; we cast off.

The original Thomas Crosby was a canoe and was used by the Methodist missionary, Thomas Crosby, who arrived in Port Simpson in Northwestern British Columbia in 1874. He did so at the invitation of the Tsimshian People and an earlier contract with the Anglican missionary William Duncan who had convinced Tsimshan People that although many aspects of his mission program were appealing, his brand of religion was too austere. Instead they preferred the more expressive version represented by the Methodist Church. Realizing that it was in their best interest to fit into the broader context of Canadian life, as they perceived it, the Tsimshian made a decision to ask the Methodist Church for a Missionary.

First Stop Port Hardy to pick up inactive polio vaccine for a baby on Mansons Landing. This time we had a reporter from The Vancouver Sun on board. He was Ken MacQueen and Harald promptly and aptly named him Clark Kent. Next day we stopped at Rivers Inlet for lunch with one of the local families. Then we set off for Mansons Landing so that I could give the baby the inactive polio immunization. Next stop was Namu, a Heiltsuk village, where I visited the Health Canada Nurse in the Clinic. Harald and Mark took off on their bikes for a quick spin. Back on board, Mark decided to make Bouillabaisse soup and we chased after some fishing boats to get some shrimp and snails. Meanwhile Dougie and Harald tried to catch a Halibut and Mark had to join in to pull it on board. This effort resulted in Mark and Harald going overboard. Luckily, we were anchored. Mark now dry was in the Galley making bread to go with the bouillabaisse and Harald and I were on the bridge sailing for Klemtu. Lunchtime came and we sat down to the scrumptious meal that Mark had prepared. I had been relishing the Bouillabaisse but Harald thought I was eating it too slowly so stuck his spoon in my plate and helped me finish it. Hopefully, this would not reach the headlines of the Vancouver Sun. Instead our group photo standing at the side of the Thomas Crosby V was on the front page of the Vancouver Sun. In Klemtu, the Native Minister of the United Church, Willie Robinson came on board for breakfast. I went and visited the clinic staff.

One day in Bella Bella the Mission Ship minister and Ken decided to take me with them in the Zodiac down to the peninsula lighthouse at Langara point. Where was Harald as this was his job? Paul and Ken were not very good at the navigation, wood stuck in the engine three times before we reached Langara Point light. On arrival, I took the head keeper aside and asked if he would make sure we could leave before dark, as I did not wish to be stuck in the strait with wood lodged in the zodiac's engine.

Green Island light was our next stop and we had quite a rocky shore to scramble up to reach the light. Meanwhile, Mark was anchored out quite a bit. After a pleasant visit with the two lighthouse keepers' families, we started back for the Crosby. Mark decided to play a silly trick and started the Crosby engines before we reached her. We finally got on board and took off our heavy safety gear.

Next stop was Ocean Falls where the clouds were right down on the water. We met with the schoolteacher and Paul arranged to hold a service in the school as the cats were still occupying the church pews. As on my last visit to Ocean Falls, I held an immunization clinic. Mrs. Archibald who ran the local hotel supplied ice cream for the children. Meanwhile, back on board the Crosby, Mark was conducting drills with the crew on how to maneuver the Crosby by reversing away and pulling along side. Off we went to Ivory Island light to visit the keepers and their families. We went to the top of the light and I pretended to jump off and fly, as it was so windy. I was given a new nickname, Nurse Ratchet from *One Flew over the Cuckoo's nest*.

We arrived at Cape Scott, which was an interesting lighthouse. The keeper showed us the colony of Rhinoceros Auklets nesting on the side of the cliff. He explained that the birds had very poor vision and used a radar system similar to bats to help them navigate. McInnes Island was another interesting stop. One of the light keeper's wives cut my hair for me. Her daughter was recording the sounds of killer whales that came by McInnes Island and the information from the recording was transmitted to University of British Columbia where it was use to identify the varying pods that traversed the area. A quick visit to Cape Mudge light and we were off to Port Simpson where there is a famous native band and there is a bandstand. The local United Church minister received us for lunch and I visited the Clinic where I would work in 2004.

Our final port of call was Prince Rupert where I contacted the Hospital in Queen Charlotte City and secured my next posting. I would start in January. Prince Rupert was the homeport of the Crosby and Harald's stepfather was the ship's inspector there. Harald took me home with him to meet his mother, Angie, and sisters, Sonja and Katherine. Off we all went to Soly's pub, the local watering hole for the mariners. My shipmates escorted me from Thomas Crosby and the entire Coast Guard Crew in Prince Rupert. Even Paul came before his flight back to Williams Lake for a Christmas break. Later Harald took me to a nightclub but boy was the music loud. Mark, Doug and I were to catch the Ferry, Queen of the North, which sunk in 2006 at Hartley Bay. The ferry arrived in Bella Bella at 5am and Mark and Doug got up to bid their nurse shipmate au revoir. I was on duty in the hospital at 8am and when I made my rounds I was not too sure if I was still at sea as I hadn't got my land legs back and I rolled from side to side as I walked down the halls. Rosemary Barrett was Jane's replacement in the medical Department. Ivor asked me if I would special my Nurse's aid as she was overdue and he wanted to induce labour. He felt that I should do the delivery, as I was the midwife. I agreed and all night long we laboured but finally McKenzie was born. I was beat and went to bed. That evening Ivor, Todd the laboratory technician and I went to the pub to wet the baby's head. Ivor asked me if I would like a bottle or paper as a thank you for helping him last night. I chose paper as Harald had already bought "Nurse Bagpipes" a couple of bottles of wine and a tease bottle of Screech for Christmas. This was a poor *newfie,* Newfoundland, joke on me as when I laughed I screeched. I would collect these in Prince Rupert en route to the Queen Charlottes. Ivor gave me a print of a sea wolf, the totem of one of the clans in Waglisla.

The next morning I was awakened by the night Nurse who said that Ivor wanted me in the operating room. This area was rarely used except in emergencies and Liz Wilson who was on holiday usually handled this area. Well I said I have not worked in an operating room for approximately 20 years. No one else here has ever done it was the answer. We had admitted a person with acute appendicitis from a cruise ship passing through the inside passage. Normally they would have been "choppered" to Vancouver but cloud was too dense. After all this is west coast rain forest country. Ivor had a specialty in anaesthetics and Don had just done his surgical refresher course. We were a team and in business. Following the surgery Ivor asked me to special the patient in the recovery phase.

Rosemary Barrett was a very accomplished pianist and we all had a great time singing Christmas carols in the hospital lounge while she played for us. Todd and I were invited to Liz Wilson's home for Christmas. Liz was married to one of the Heiltsuk Nation and their son was at University of British Columbia studying law. We had a lovely time. Todd and I spent New Year's Eve together and I brought him my television to look after. Harald would pick up my television on the Crosby's next visit to Waglisla. Next day I left on the Queen of the North for Prince Rupert on my way to my new job in Queen Charlotte City on the Queen Charlotte Islands.

Chapter 3

ᔕ

QUEEN CHARLOTTE ISLANDS

HARALD MET me when I arrived in Prince Rupert and we drove to his home where Angie, Al, Sonja and Katherine were pleased to see me. Angie had a lovely German style brunch waiting. Pork and steak tartar was something that I had never eaten. I certainly did enjoy it and the pickled herring. I managed to revive my German, which surprisingly came back from my days learning the language at Glasgow University. There was little time, as I had to catch the next ferry to the "Charlottes".

I arrived in the "Charlottes" and took the only taxi to the hospital and luckily there were not too many people waiting for it. I collected my key for the trailer next door to the hospital and unpacked. Next day I went to work and received my day shift orientation. All the nursing staff was on call except for myself. We all had a variety of roles to play in this type of patient care setting. Some patients were acutely sick and some were elderly and required assistance in feeding and bathing. The nurse's assignment for the shift included a mixture of situations including the labour and delivery room or the emergency room along with two acute care patients and two elderly patients. At times, this made things rather tricky if you were bathing an elderly patient in the bath tub and you had to take off for an emergency cardiac admission that had arrived in the out patient area. Next day I had my orientation to the night shift. Halfway through the shift we admitted a woman in labour. Neither of my two colleagues felt comfortable in dealing with this situation so I ended my orientation leading the way. We called the doctor who wanted to wait for second stage, as this was a third pregnancy. "Have you looked out side as it is snowing quite heavily"? So down the doctor came to the hospital. He was grateful that we had alerted him as he lived at the top of a steep hill. The Queen Charlotte Islands is home to the Haida Nation. Haida Gwaii is the Haida Nation word for the Queen Charlotte Islands. The Queen Charlotte Islands were not covered in ice during the last glaciation but were a refuga for many species of plants and animals. One of the few species of worms that are native to British Columbia is found here. The Queen Charlotte Island's bear is another sub species of black bear that live here and no where else in the world. It is slightly larger than the other Black Bear that live in British Columbia.

Later that week, I rented a car and drove down to Masset where Jane was working for the Health Care Society and the Canadian Armed Forces Base. On the way I passed the famous Golden Spruce tree, which was a unique yellow coloured spruce tree and was protected from logging. Unfortunately, someone cut it down and despite efforts to produce another golden spruce all efforts have been in vain. Jane and I went to explore Massett. We went to the Anglican Church on the Reserve and Jane played the organ and I sang. The Priests were dressed in Button Blanket Regalia. Afterwards we explored the Coast and visited the Base hospital. Jane and I made arrangements for me to buy her car in a couple of weeks.

In a couple of weeks, Harald arrived with my television that he had picked up from Todd in Bella Bella and transported it to Prince Rupert on the Crosby. The snow was falling thickly on the ground and it was difficult to get reception on many channels. We called the television station and were informed that if we wished reception we would have to take a broom and sweep the snow off the satellite dish. We chose to do without the television.

Next day, we rented a car and set off for Masset to collect Jane's Volkswagen. We had spent the evening with Jane and her partner in the Pink Panther pool hall. We stayed in a beautiful sea front lodge where the waves would lull us to sleep. This Chief who owned the lodge had waited up for us like a father figure head.

Back at Queen Charlotte City, I was getting bored even though I had only been there for a couple of months and decided that it was time to look for other work. I had an offer of a Community Health position in

Atikameg, Alberta where there was a Whooping Cough epidemic, which had been raging there in the 18 year old population for over a year.

I booked my passage on the Ferry which would take me to Prince Rupert where Harald would join me and then we would take the ferry from there to Port Hardy and drive to Victoria. I worked my last night shift handed in the trailer key, packed the car and set off for the dock. When I reached the ferry dock there was no sign of the ferry. I called Harald and the ferry had been held up owing to very high seas. I waited in my sleepless stupor but still no ferry. At 3 PM. I decided I had better go into the village to the only restaurant and have some lunch. Still on weather hold, I ate my Chinese meal and during that time a nurse who I had worked with from Holland came in and offered me a bed in her home. By dinnertime, the weather had still not let up so I took the kind lady out for dinner. Next morning, the ferry was to sail at 10 am. I had a lovely breakfast of strong coffee and blueberry pancakes served on the famous Dutch blue delft patterned china. I bid my gracious colleague a very grateful farewell and boarded the ferry for Prince Rupert. Harald met me at the terminal and we headed to Solly's for dinner where the Crosby crew and the coastguard were waiting. Angie had a bed all ready for me and the next day Harald and I went to get my airline ticket to Victoria as I no longer had time to take a ferry and drive home. I had to get to Atikameg. I left my car with Harald. I almost missed the flight as the airport bus had left from the terminal pick up point. The airport in Prince Rupert is on Digby Island and there is a special ferry to take one there. Harald luckily knows the small boat operator and in spike high heels, I fled down a steep ramp to catch the small transport boat.

Chapter 4

ᖒ

ATIKAMEG ALBERTA

IN MARCH 1990, I started a 6-week assignment in Atikameg Alberta.
I flew to Ft. St John and was met by the charter pilot who flew me to
High Prairie, Alberta. As Atikameg Health Centre had no lodgings, I
stayed in a motel in High Prairie. Whitefish Lake First Nation (Atikameg),
which means Little Whitefish, is located 200 miles north of Edmonton
near Little Slave Lake. The Whitefish Lake First Nation is Cree. The drive
was an hour each way and the Nurse in charge would pick me up and
another Nurse Wendy from Red Deer, Alberta and take us to the Health
Centre. Wendy was only there for a short spell.

The next nurse to come was Jim. None of the other nurses had ever
done public health before and this made contact tracing a little more difficult. There was plenty of snow on the road and one day while driving
back from the health center, Jim put the truck into the ditch and we had
to get a tow truck to get us out. Another day, we were joined by the nurse
from Sucker Lake and drove to Faller for a slap up meal. Faller is the capital of this region and has a beautiful cathedral. The rail track runs through
the center of the town of High Prairie. The rail tracks are surrounded by
grain elevators which are tall, stately erections that can be seen for miles
on the Canadian prairie's flat landscape. The Prairie Provinces are known
as Canadian's wheat basket as the main agricultural product on the prairies is wheat. While in High Prairie, I received a call from the Kitikmeot
Health Board in Cambridge Bay offering me another contract. When I
finished my six weeks in Atikameg, I had already accepted a short-term

contract to work in Watson Lake in the Yukon until the end of April 1990. I returned to my home in Victoria for a few days and then I was off to Watson Lake. I would go to revisit Cambridge Bay in mid May where it would be 24-hour daylight.

Chapter 5

᧡

WATSON LAKE YUKON TERRITORY

Watson Lake 10 Kilometres from the southern border of the Yukon and the Northern border of British Columbia was named after Frank Watson, a Gold seeker from Lake Tahoe, California, who settled there in 1898.

According to oral tradition, the original inhabitants of the area, Kaska-Dena, were seasonal migrants traveling within their territory while hunting and gathering food supplies. The Kaska people lived in the mountainous headwaters of the Pelly and Liard Rivers in the eastern Yukon. The area of the Liard First Nation extended to Upper Liard, Frances, and Highland rivers and extended into the upper Pelly drainage in the north to the Dease River in the southwest. Lower Post was the main settlement. They hunted caribou, moose and Dall sheep and traded furs with coastal Indians. Around 1945, the Department of Indian Affairs began building settlements for the native people; Upper Liard became the Liard River First Nation community and in 1961, the five Kaska First Nations amalgamated into the Liard Indian First Nation. There are approximately 891 band members registered with the department of Indian Affairs in Ottawa.

Watson Lake is on a gravel highway that links the Yukon to Alaska and was built after the Second World War by American war veterans. Watson Lake is an incorporated town, regional service and business centre for the area and many First Nations people live there and in the surrounding communities of Two-Mile and Two and a Half Mile. Forestry and energy exploration add to the economic growth. Sa Dena Hes, a lead -zinc mine, opened in 1991 and employed First Nations people until the closure in 1993. At the present time the mine is currently employing a small number of people.

In March 1990, I arrived at the small hospital and was shown my room. The sleeping and living quarters for the staff were an extension of the hospital. My colleagues were Joan whom I was replacing and Maurice. Both these people I would encounter again in 1993 at Dalhousie University in Halifax, Nova Scotia. There was a permanent Nurse, Dianne, who lived in the community. The doctor was Saaid and he was quite the character. He would go gold panning and then use his spoils to make jewelry for the staff. We had an emergency room and delivery room. The nursing staff was responsible for the laboratory and x-rays. Most of the inpatients were on intravenous treatments for either alcohol related gastric disease or acute infections. In the daytime there were two nurses on duty and one on the night shift. At night between 2 am and 7 am there were no Royal Canadian Mounted Police, RCMP, on duty so one was literally on ones own. Many summer visitors traveled the gravel highway between British Columbia to Alaska. Due to the variance of the gravel road surface and the paved roads in the South, many accidents are brought into Watson Lake hospital.

One day Dianne asked me if I would like to go to Liard Hot Springs. *Yes, it sounds like a great idea.* Off we went driving along beside the Liard River with the Cassiar Mountains looming in the distance. The springs were beautifully warm and in winter the alder trees that over hang the pool are all frost covered and sparkling from the steam lifting off the sulphur smelling water.

Another day the Community Health Canada Nurse drove me down to Lower Post. It was 11 in the morning and everyone was asleep including some lying on the dirt road. Alcohol abuse is a very bad health problem in this area.

One of Maurice's real dreads was that a pregnant woman would come in while he was alone on night duty. Well it happened and he coped well because he had requested that if this event happened he wished to come and get me to do the initial assessment. Well he waited until I was on shift and Dianne requested that she go in with the labouring woman. Saaid has started a syntocin drip. So I left Dianne and Saaid, Maurice went to bed and I dealt with my other patients. I heard the baby cry and all was well or so I thought. When Saaid screamed from the room *Annette help*! When I arrived he had his hand stuck in the patient and the uterus had clamped down on his hand. I used my midwifery knowledge and used a Créde's maneuver to expel a retained placenta but this time it include the physician's hand. It worked well and the physician's blue hand soon became pink again. A lesson had been learned, caution on the use of syntocin and let Mother Nature do her thing. Now it was my turn for some fun on duty. It was around 3 am and two First Nations Young men who were very drunk came in demanding attention, as was their right. I told them I had other patients to see to first and please fill out your admission forms. Some blue tones followed and my response was I do not care if you are a Kangaroo; I have other patients I must deal with. The one fellow had a small laceration on his hand which required stitching and was already covered with a bandage. I checked on my other patients, called the doctor in and then checked the tetanus immunization card. An anti tetanus dose was required and I dealt with this in the emergency room. The doctor, a relief person, came in to do the suturing. I was busy assisting the doctor when suddenly the doctor thumbed on the man's chest as if he was about to start CPR, Cardio Pulmonary resuscitation. Leave my nurse alone he said to the young man. The patient was poking at me under the drapes. Suturing over and all was quiet. The two men left, as did the relief doctor. I went and checked on my other patients and when I came back to my desk there were two women smelling strongly of alcohol, fighting and pulling at each other's hair; they were a mother and her daughter. The daughter threw the mother's snow boots out into the cold. I had to be firm. "Ladies this is a hospital". What are you doing here? Are you sick? "No". I asked the daughter to get her mother's snow boots back and go home, as I really did not want to have to call out the RCMP. The two women cooperated with my request and away home they went.

Time to leave Watson Lake for a brief sojourn in Victoria before journeying to Cambridge Bay.

Chapter 6

ᕐ

CAMBRIDGE BAY REVISITED MAY 1990

I FLEW FROM Victoria via Canadian Airlines and on to Edmonton to over night at the Nisku Inn. The Nisku Inn has a bus to transfer passengers from the airport to the motel. The driver was a lady who immediately asked where was I from. I knew she was originally from the east of Scotland. I told her that I came from Aberdeen and she immediately branched into broad Buchan to the amazement of the other passengers who did not understand this foreign language. "Foo ye deein"(how are you)? Reply "Nae bad a'va" (not bad at all). There was more but I won't bother you with all the patter.

After a delightful swim, and dinner I bedded down for the night as I already had one hour of a time change and had to be ready for an early start.

In the morning, I was off to the municipal airport and aboard another Canadian Airline bound for Yellowknife. The service on the northern route far excels that of the southern flights. Business Class for all with a choice of entrée, which is usually arctic char or musk ox and the proverbial Eskimo pie. All alcoholic and non-alcoholic beverages are gratis. Milk is a popular, exotic drink with adults and children alike as it is not available in the smaller Arctic communities except in cans or powdered. We touched down in Yellowknife and waited for the next leg of the journey to Cambridge Bay. We were off again and the jet touched down in Cambridge Bay and there was good old Jimmy. *"Solomon Bar, Annette".* He grabbed my luggage and we were off in the truck to the Health Centre.

Susan was in the throws of moving the nurses' residence to a new three-story building across the street. My first task would be to help with the move. The new residence was shared with the single office government workers who worked normal office hours and held social activities after these hours. We worked on call hours and sometimes needed peace and quiet to catch up sleep.

In the North water is a precious commodity. Dishes and laundry are not done daily nor does one run the tap for cold water. It pays to be an early bird so as not to be left in the shower in the morning when the tank has run out of water and you are left wearing soap and shampoo! When we lived next to, or above the health center, the water tank was always kept topped up by the water truck driver. The actual apartments were rather well furnished and I was house rent free in the transient suite, which was used by visiting health care professionals. The rent-free deal is long gone and in 1995 rents for all jumped to $ 800 - $1000 per month. Salaries did not keep pace.

The two Eva were still there and so were Valerie, Rachel and Brian. We had a new dental therapist Shirley. Susan was about to go out on leave and there were two brand new nurses on their way up for orientation. Iona was off on holiday and then on to maternity leave. Valerie too was ready for her vacation and we would meet later on that summer in Pelly Bay before she left to study medicine at McMaster University in September. Colleen and June arrived from Ontario and Edmonton respectively. Susan would do the initial orientation and Rachel would help Colleen and I would take June under my wing. Susan went on holiday and Rachel took Colleen on the fly in day trip to Bay Chimo and Bathhurst Inlet clinics. Unfortunately, the trip was extended to 5 days due to inclement weather conditions. This left me on call for 5 straight days plus orientating June. The transition to out post nursing from hospital nursing is a whole different conceptual framework. One has to listen to the history, examine, diagnose, prescribe, treat and know how to perform the appropriate laboratory test and necessary X rays. One has to know when to refer when the situation is no longer in one's scope of practice. One also has to get to know who is who in the community and where to get resources.

All this takes time to learn and we were definitely understaffed in a 5 nurse, nursing station. On Colleen and Rachel's return, I met them at the dock and said *"Hi guys"*; "I am beat you are on call". Flexibility is the name of the game. Off I went to bed.

One day June and I went for a walk on the tundra. It was nesting time and unknowingly we got too close to the Jaeger's nest and we were dive bombed by one of the Jaegers. Every fourth year is a boom year for lemmings, the favourite food of the ookpik, the snowy owl. In that space of time, there are more snowy owl chicks and this keeps the lemming population in check. Lemmings do perform "the run over the cliff "when their population does not have sufficient food.

The beer line dance was on and Rachel finally called and said she was beat and that there was a man coming in with a possible Collis fracture. "*Ok* I will take over." "*Sleep well and see you in the afternoon at the clinic*".

The presence of alcohol in a community makes such a difference to the accident rate and how busy the nurse is kept. Rachel and Colleen were called out one night to a gunshot wound at a campsite on the tundra. The man was still wielding a gun and was very inebriated. When they returned, I asked them what is the number one rule in first aid? No one got this answer right. The correct answer is to maker sure the first aid person is safe. When one is called out on this type of call, one should notify a colleague and the RCMP. The next incident was an 8-month-old child who had been sent out to Yellowknife with respiratory distress of unknown origin. The hospital kept her a few days but could not diagnose the cause. She was sent back to Cambridge Bay at 4 PM that afternoon and was dead by 8 PM. Rachel and Colleen got the call from the frantic parents and called June and I for back up. When I reached the door of the Nursing Station, Rachel and Colleen were performing CPR in front of the door. I unlocked the door helped them in and ran up stairs to get the oxygen and sent June to get the tracheotomy set. All to no avail as the child had been dead in her crib before she had been brought to the health center. In the end the diagnosis was sudden infant death syndrome, which we now know, in some instances is associated with smoking. After some tea and discussion, I sent the staff home and the family members were taken care of by their relatives. Three days later the hamlet was closed and everyone attended the church service at the Anglican Church. Following the service, all the Inuit went to the graveyard and we returned to the health centre. The service was accompanied by very loud mourning sounds.

A few days following the funeral, Shirley decided that she was going fishing for Arctic Char in the river up the road a little way. Shirley was a Cree Indian and did not need a fishing license as we would. So June and I joined her to watch and left Rachael and Colleen on call. On our way to the river, we suddenly hear a loud bang and noticed black smoke coming from the direction of the airstrip. Not long ago the scheduled flight had flown over us. Could there have been a crash? While we were out walking on the tundra via the dirt road, the RCMP truck went whizzing by us and did not even wave. This was odd. They were going towards the summer fish camps. I said to June and Shirley, *I think I had better go back to town.* When I reached the nursing station the population of Cambridge Bay was around the building. "What happened"? "There has been an explosion". Five teenagers had been sniffing propane down at the dock and then decided to have a smoke. Two had become cinders and another had run into the ocean to put out the flames. The surviving three, two boys and a girl were in the nursing station Brian, Rachel and Colleen were there. The smell of burning flesh is something one never forgets. Brian asked me to *man the phones.* We are awaiting news of three medivac planes to take the victims to the burns unit in Edmonton. The three planes arrived and took the patients to Edmonton for skin grafting. To this day, these teenagers will not forget what happened as they still have some scarring.

Next day I received a call from the agency I had been working for who requested that I represent them in a competition for a nursing post on the coast guard's Icebreaker. *"Ok that sounds like a fun job".* An interview in Victoria was required. Unfortunately, I could not go away as that would leave Cambridge Bay short staffed and I was on a contract. Health Canada decided that a telephone interview would suffice. The interview had many questions pertaining to life aboard a ship. Thank goodness for the experience on board the Thomas Crosby V. This competition was across Canada. I won it hands down but the agency lost the posting as they put too high a bid in for my salary. Jacinth Tremble from Health Canada told me to come and see her when I was home in Victoria. I was rather sad that I could not join the coast guard. The coast guard's ship, Sir Wilfred Laurier was in Cambridge Bay that summer.

One day, when things were quiet and Valerie was back, Rachel, Colleen, June and my self went for a walk round the ice-free Bay to see the ship wreck which had belonged to the early explorer Roland Amundsen. It's remains stuck out of the water. On the opposite shore was the first old stone church in the region.

Susan came back from vacation and I went home to Victoria on my break. I went to see Jacinth Tremble from Health Canada *"when the next competition for the nurse on an icebreaker is advertised you apply on your own and not through an agency".*

Two weeks later, I was back to the Nisku Inn in Edmonton then on to Yellowknife and back in Cambridge Bay where I relieved Susan from call duty. There had been a baby with diarrhea in the clinic earlier in the day and Susan thought I could call the mother in the afternoon to see if all was well. I did call the mother and all was well and the baby was feeding without any problems. We were getting ready for a farewell dinner for Jean, the chief executive officer of the Kitikmeot Health Board, who was going out on maternity leave in two days time on the next scheduled flight. Her family had already left for the south in Saskatchewan and she had moved into the transient suite with me. At 5 am, I received a call from the mother of the baby with diarrhea saying that she now had gas pains and demanding that I make a house call. I advised her that she should try some flat ginger ale. At 7 a.m., another call from the same party demanding a house call. I said that I would go and check all the family's files and would call them following this task. Upon reviewing the charts, only the baby had been seen at the clinic. I called the family and the dad answered the phone, yes the ginger ale worked. Back at the residence Jean could not believe that such a fuss was made over gas pains. Next night, it was Jean's turn to have gas pains. Around 5 a.m. a little voice called from the bedroom next to mine. *"Aunty Nettie, I am not sure if I have gas pains or not."* I got up and went to Jean's room and suggested that perhaps she could try a warm bath and see what happens. I went into the living room and downed a wake up coffee. 5.30 a.m. Jean came out and said I am not really sure what is happening. I thought, this is Jean's second baby so I think we will go to the clinic and see what is happening. Jean was due to fly to Saskatchewan that afternoon to have her baby in a couple of weeks. *"Before you go across do you have anything in the laundry room"?* "Yes", said Jean, and I whisked down and picked the laundry up and put it into Jean's suitcase. *"I will just go to the bathroom"*, Jean said. *"I will give Brian a call".* Brian lived next door to the apartment block. While I was talking to Brian a voice from the bathroom called out *"my water just broke".* I passed the message to Brian and he said he would see us across the way. Jean and I left the apartment and got to the first of three flights of stairs. Jean stopped. This was the first recognizable contraction. That over we went down the next flight of stairs.

The contractions were strong and coming every two minutes. We made it to the delivery room. Jean said, *"I have to push"*. *"Hop onto the bed"*, I said, as I heard the door. *"Brian"*, I called, *"she is pushing"*. I flung open a pair of gloves and delivery pack and by 6.30 am we had a lovely little girl. I put on the kettle and we all had a cup of tea. *"No muss no fuss"*, said Brian, *"the best type of delivery"*. Jean was my boss so I felt more at a distance when Brian did the delivery. Jean phoned her husband, Ron and gave him the good news. At 8.30 am, I called over to Jerry's house. Jerry had three children and was replacing Jean. *"Are you making breakfast"*? *"Yes"*. *"Well I have a patient in the clinic could you bring over a plate"*? *"Sure"*. Over came Jerry and to her amazement there was mum and babe. Later on, Jean came back to the apartment and I helped her with the babe. Flights were rearranged and Jean and new babe went home. I was to meet up with Jean and Ron in 1994 on the DEW line, the radar early warning systems, operated by Canada and United States.

One of my greatest dreads was to have a very young infant come to the clinic with RSV, Respiratory Syncytical Virus. This is an acute lower respiratory tract infection associated with symptoms of a cough, and wheezing. The most common clinical presentation of RSV in young children is bronchiolitis, which is inflammation of the small tissues in the lungs. The younger the child, the narrower the airway and in a very small baby, the airway is the diameter of a drinking straw. The airway rapidly closes with the viral secretions and immediate medivac intervention is required before the airway is closed. The child is required to go to the hospital in Edmonton from this part of the Arctic for intensive care with oxygen supplementation, intravenous fluids, and other supportive care. My dread was realized when one evening a two month old child was brought to the clinic. I was in luck as the weather was good and Willy had his plane in Cambridge Bay. The child was 2 months old and when the parents brought her to the clinic, you could hear the wheezing as she came through the clinic doors. No need for a stethoscope. I set up the oxygen and gave some metered ventolin to dilate the respiratory tract. I called Willy and he was ready to fly to Edmonton. I called Ramona as the escort medivac nurse as she had recently come from the pediatric intensive care unit to work in Cambridge Bay. The child recovered and was back in Cambridge Bay in three weeks.

One day when Valerie was on call Rachel asked me if I would go on a bike ride? I had not been on a bike for about ten years and besides I didn't have one. "We can borrow one from one of the teachers". That decided, we set off on the tundra. No, there are no roads, just rocks and sand. It was a warm day and the mosquitoes hovered over ones head like an enormous cloud. We had on long sleeved blouses and jeans, but the space between the jeans and our socks and our blouses and gloves were attractive targets for the bloodsuckers. The wild life on the tundra always fascinated me. Some species like the musk ox and the willow ptarmigan had survived the last ice age and some have not, such as the saber-toothed tiger. The willow ptarmigan is a very small bird and lives on willow shoots and the like. They adapt to the environment by changing their feathers to match the surroundings. In the winter, they are white to match the snow, at melt up they are patchy brown and white and in the summer they are predominantly brown to match the tundra. One can approach a flock and pick one up, as they seem to have no fear of humans. While out on the tundra, we saw a herd of musk oxen. The adults circled around the youngsters to protect them. Six hours later, I alighted from the bike and I think my legs had forgotten what terra firma was.

A few days later, Susan decided to have us all over for supper. I was on call and Susan had seen Jeannie at the prenatal clinic that day. She is 32 weeks gestation and it was her fourth baby. She had an obstetrical history with her other three pregnancies of going into premature labour. If you get a call from Jeannie get the magnesium sulphate going. I did receive a call, but luckily it was a child with sore ears. I left Susan's house and walked to the clinic only to find that my keys wouldn't open the door as my key was bent with over use. One of the other nurses came and opened the clinic door and I got the spare one from the key box inside. I saw the sick child and went back to Susan's house. After a pleasant evening we all went home. At one am the phone rang, it was Jeannie phoning from the phone outside the nursing station door. All people in Cambridge Bay do not have phones and this particular phone only connects to the nurse on call. Over to the clinic I went only to find out Jeannie had been in labour since 11 PM. She was in full-blown labour. I started an Intravenous but it was too late for Magnesium Sulphate to stop the labour. Nature had beaten me this time. I called for a medivac. The weather was great but there were no planes available. The circuit court judge had taken a plane and the other one was out on a call somewhere in another part of the Arctic. A baby at 32 weeks has problem with breathing due to underdevelopment of the lungs and requires assistance to breathe in a special incubator. The heart and lungs are not ready to function in the world outside the mother's womb. In the North the rule is to have pregnant women sent off to Yellowknife at 38 weeks so that complications can be dealt with in a hospital environment. I called Susan and told her that Jeannie was in full-blown labour and that I could not get a medivac. I need to stay in the room with Jeannie. Could you please come in and man the phone as the Hospital Nursing Supervisor in Yellowknife is trying to get us a medivac. All premature labours go to Edmonton, as that is the nearest intensive care nursery unit to Cambridge Bay. Brian was not in the community, but even if he was, we do not have the complex equipment necessary for dealing with this situation. Susan arrived and the labour progressed slowly but steadily and all was well. Stanton found a team with equipment and the pilot was ready to take off as soon as the medivac plane returned from Edmonton with another premature labour from Yellowknife. Second stage was nearing. We had amongst our nursing team, Ramona who had recently come on staff from the pediatric intensive care unit in Edmonton. Ramona can look after the babe and get the umbilical catheter in place. This is the easiest route to access a vein and for starting intravenous therapy on a premature babe. I'll do the delivery. Over came Ramona. I was preparing for the delivery when the plane landed. Both mother and baby were stable. Mother stayed in Cambridge Bay with the three other children and the babe went to Edmonton with the medivac team. I went to bed and came back to work at noon.

The next day, the base commander at Cam Main invited us for dinner at the DEW line camp at the Cambridge Bay site. The men that work in the early warning radar system are well catered to by international chefs and top of the line food comparable to a cruise ship. We gladly accepted his kind invitation, as this was one way to maintain ones sanity in the wilds. We all enjoyed the outing and little did I know that I would have three weeks of this scrumptious food in 1994.

A few days later, Rachel and I were to be the next medivac team. 4.30 in the afternoon a severely injured man was brought into the nursing station. The man had been guiding the backing up sewage truck, which had slipped and hit him in the upper part of his thigh. He was in severe shock. At 5 pm we set off for Yellowknife expecting to meet the jet to take the man to Edmonton, which was the nearest surgical orthopedic unit. We soon discovered that we were the team to transport this man to Edmonton. We had almost used all our intravenous supplies and our morphine en route from Cambridge Bay to Yellowknife. We could not continue the journey without these as our patient was in severe shock and was bleeding from a dangerous site; the femoral artery was sliced. His blood pressure was very low and he must have had a great deal of pain. The Inuit as a nation are very stoic people. We called John who ran the Kitikmoet Boarding home in Yellowknife where patients from the Kitkmoet region awaiting hospital admission or discharge or specialist appointments stay. John arrived and sped me off to the hospital and on the way we radioed in our supply request. The nursing supervisor met us at the door armed with the supplies. *"Don't you want to know the patient's name for the morphine so that you can record it in your narcotic records"*? *"Ok"* and away we went back to continue our journey to Edmonton. We had lightning strikes all the way to Edmonton and there were times when the patient's blood pressure was so low that we thought we had lost him. As the plane touched down in Edmonton, he sat up and watched us land. To watch the expression on the man's face, one would never guess that he had been so close to death's door many times on this journey. It was midnight and the ambulance was waiting for us. It took us to the Royal Alex emergency department and the man was in surgery having his leg amputated within the hour. Rachael and I took a taxi with our oxygen tank and medivac bags to a restaurant for some dinner. We received some odd looks from some of the other patrons. At 2 am, we took off for Yellowknife and this time we had a different set of patients to escort. There were three Inuit, one woman and two men and a Dene elder going back to Fort Simpson who did not speak a word of Inuktitut or English. He was full of tubes and was trying to pull these out. He was very restless so we thought it best to have him lie on the floor, rather than on two seats, to prevent him falling and hurting himself. At 4 am, we landed in Fort Simpson and the elder was transferred to the ambulance and to people who could speak his language. At 5 am, we arrived in Yellowknife and there was John to pick up the Inuit people and Rachel and I. John dropped us at the Yellowknife Inn and we hit the sack. I woke up at 9 am and left Rachel asleep. My mission was to get some fresh fruit and vegetable and go to a bank machine. We had to be back at the airport to meet René so I hustled around, did my shopping and went back to the Yellowknife Inn to wake Rachel. While she dressed, I ate breakfast. And then we took a taxi to the airport, as John was busy with patient transportation. We took off for Cambridge Bay. Back at the Nursing Station Susan sent us to bed.

Next day the nurse from the coast guard icebreaker, *Sir Wilfred Laurier,* came to the clinic to invite us to a cocktail party on board the following evening. This Nurse was on the ship that I should have been on having won the competition. I did not let on to the nurse about the situation. I thought, I must get an Arctic Char to have the coastguard take to Prince Rupert and give it to Al, Harald's stepfather. This would be much easier than trying to keep it frozen on my flight home via Edmonton to Victoria and then up to Prince Rupert. After work I hopped down to the Hunters and Trappers shop and bought an Arctic Char that I wrapped and it was ready for the next evening to take it to the icebreaker. When I arrived at the dock there were many people waiting for the zodiac to take them to the ship. The (Royal Canadian Mounted Police) RCMP invited me to sit and wait in their truck as they too were going to the party. There were far too many people going to the ship so I asked if RCMP would take the fish to the ship and explain that it had to go to Al in Prince Rupert. That worked out well as the captain had the chef take care of the Artic Char. A few weeks later, Harald phoned and said his mother was delighted with the fish and all the family had enjoyed it.

Back on call, I received a radio call from the lay dispenser in Bay Chimo. A middle-aged man who had never had mumps in childhood thought that he had mumps. It is much better for men to have mumps in childhood. When adult males have mumps, there is a great deal of pain and swelling in the genitals. I had to be creative in answering the call as the whole world hears what is said and most people have the radio on round the clock. Treat the fever, pain and swelling with Tylenol 500 milligrams every 6 hours until the symptoms have gone. I was scheduled to go to Bay Chimo and Bathurst Inlet in a few days to do the "well women clinic", chronic disease reviews and immunizations. I would check on the man then and meantime if there were problems, the lay dispenser would radio.

Willie was waiting at the airstrip and off I went to do the clinics first in Bay Chimo. The community is a very traditional Inuit settlement of 20 people, no running water except for a pipe down the center of the hamlet and no electric power in the clinic. While I was waiting for the generator to be hooked up, I bought a beautiful canoe made of seal leather. Sitting in the seal skin canoe was soapstone carved man dressed in seal fur. I also bought a drum dancer clad in sealskin and carved from soapstone with a drum in his hand. I was ready to start my clinic and one had to be inventive. The clinic had no examination table and to do the well woman check, the patient sat in a chair and I sat opposite her. Her feet were on my chair and hence the laboratory slides were taken.

Next stop was Bathhurst Inlet, which had a population of 60 people and a similar environment to Bay Chimo.

Back to Cambridge Bay just in time for Brian to make us musk ox stew and home made bread. Brian was soon to retire to Salt Spring Island near Victoria, British Columbia. He told us all that this was probably the only time that we would eat musk ox stew with out any of the beast's hair in the stew.

The word frozen usually conjures up a cold scene or person. One day a woman called me and told me that her husband was frozen in the shower. He had bent down to pick up the soap and could not stand up again. I went to the home and gave the man an injection of Diazepam. In a few minutes he was able to move and leave his prison.

Then I had to pack as I was going back to Pelly Bay for a few months. Jimmy was at the ready and whisked me to the airstrip. I would be back to Cambridge Bay on my way home to Victoria.

Chapter 7

๛

PELLY BAY MY FAVOURITE COMMUNITY

N OLD Artic Legend: The Inuit dogs stood at the gates of heaven and when an Inuit hunter who was good to his dogs came to the gates, the dogs wagged their tails and welcomed him into heaven. But when an Inuit hunter who beat and starved his dogs came to the gates, the dogs growled and he was forced to wander the ice-covered tundra for eternity.

I arrived in Pelly Bay and Mike came to pick me up and take me to the clinic. Katherine Teresa, Gaeton and Cora were there and another nurse, Margaret, who would be there for a short while. Cora was leaving in a few days for Grise Fiord and Paula would stay a short while. I was very glad to be back in my favourite community as it is so much more traditional than others, given that it is only accessible by air. A new member had joined the health care team and that was Gabriel, the community health representative. Everyone was happy to see me again. I went off to the coop after clinic and met Agnes who does not speak English. She shook me by two hands not one, which is a symbol of respect. She, like many other older women had a baby in her Amuiti on her back under her parka. The baby was her daughter's child. It is the custom in Pelly Bay for the daughter to give her mother one of her children. The child then is "custom adopted" by the grandmother and when the child is old enough, she learns who her birth mother is. In the Arctic, a woman is not a woman unless she has a baby in the parka on her back. The same goes for a sister. If one sister has six children and her sister cannot conceive then the seventh baby will be given to her sister and "custom adopted". When the child is old enough then she will learn who her birth mother is. Pelly Bay is the only community that I know of that still carries on this tradition.

Cora left for Grise Fiord on the same plane that Paula came in on. Paula had been in New Delhi and had worked with Mother Teresa with the outcasts so we heard lots of interesting stories from this area of the world. The police had arrested Paula because of her work with Mother Teresa. Paula also had two very bad experiences. One with gastrointestinal sickness and the other with malaria; she had almost died from both these illnesses. Margaret was on call on her last night in Pelly Bay. Before, leaving on the plane she reported that a middle-aged woman had called her out during the night with a severe headache and fever and that she had given her Tylenol with codeine. I thanked her for the information and said I would go with Gabriel to see the woman at home. Gabriel had to help translate for me. We said good-bye to Margaret and wished her well in her next venture working in India.

Gabriel and I set off for the woman's house walking down the road, Gabriel told me about a husky pup that had been kicked in the head by a man and could I please help the puppy. I said I would be glad to help after we had visited the patient. When we arrived at the house the woman was in poor shape. I called Mike for the taxi an open backed truck to transport the woman to the clinic. I called Paula to warn her of the patient's imminent arrival.

Gabriel and I went round the corner to look at the two-week-old husky pup. The pup was suffering badly with irreversible injuries. Gabriel wanted me to put the pup to sleep with sodium Phenobarbital the substance that veterinarians use to put animals to sleep. *"Gabriel, I cannot use sodium Phenobarbital for an animal because the drug is on the narcotic register and under the Canadian Criminal Code". "I must simultaneously write the dose and patient's name in the narcotic book, and in the patient's medical record". "It would be kinder to shoot the pup". "Can you please ask someone do this"? "We must get back to the clinic".*

Back at the clinic, some men in the community pitched in to unload the stretcher from the taxi into the clinic. After assessing the patient and setting up an Intravenous solution of normal saline, I called the doctor in Yellowknife and told him the patient's signs, symptoms. My diagnosis was disseminated intravascular clotting (DIC) and that we would need a medivac team. *Don't be ridiculous,* that can't be the diagnosis but I will send the medivac. There is no cure for DIC and the patient's condition deteriorated before our eyes. The medivac team arrived and off they took for Yellowknife and despite the medivac nurse's best efforts, the patient died as the plane landed in Yellowknife. The doctor met the plane and sent the body to Edmonton for autopsy. The doctor telephoned us with the sad news, which had to be passed on to the deceased woman's husband.

Gabriel and I went to the husband's home where we relayed the sad news in English and Inuktituk. Afterwards Gabriel mentioned that he did not know how I was able to do this type of work. I didn't do this alone we did it together.

Now the hamlet would prepare for the funeral. The whole hamlet closed for the funeral and everyone in the community went to the church. The service was Catholic and in Inuktitut. There was no loud mourning or wailing and everyone lined up to bless the body at the end of the service. Out of respect for the community members, I was at the end of the line. As everyone was wearing parkas, it was difficult to see what I was supposed to do when handed the gold stick containing Holy Water. So I chose to make the sign of the cross over the body by flicking the golden object in the four directions of the cross. After the service had totally concluded, the hamlet members all went to the graveyard on the hill for the burial. Paula and I went back to the clinic.

The doctor phoned Paula with the result of the recent autopsy. The cause of death confirmed DIC. Paula told the doctor that he owed me an apology. This happened on his next visit from Yellowknife. We no longer had Brian in Cambridge Bay and as yet we had no replacement doctor in the Kitikmoet region.

The following morning, the snow had almost left the hamlet and I heard the most awful racket of gulls crying. These clever birds had come to clean up the mess of litter under the snow. When Katherine arrived at work I asked her if the gulls came every year. *"Yes, and they will be here for 48 hours until the hamlet is clean and then they will go to the garbage dump for the rest of the summer."* Night and day these birds cried and why not it was 24-hour daylight.

Two elders from Pelly Bay had appeared in the movie *Never Cry Wolf* from the book of the same name by Farley Mowatt. By the time I was in Pelly Bay only the wife was still alive. I met her while home visiting with Gabriel. She showed me the charcoal herring bone style markings on her legs, which long ago were a symbol of beauty. I have two Inuit dolls in my collection from Coppermine who have the same design on their faces.

A team of Japanese anthropologists arrived in Pelly Bay and went out on the islands with the elders to learn about the old ways. The dogs are let off on the islands for the summer, as they are no longer needed for going on the frozen tundra.

Annette Hart was in the later stages of pregnancy and she took Paula and I out on the tundra on her all terrain vehicle (ATV) to visit the water reservoir. We were all enjoying the jaunt until the ATV rolled over and we all went down a slope. I thought, as we rolled down, I better be prepared for a delivery on the tundra. All was well and we all scrambled back up to the ATV none the worse for our unexpected trip down the incline. Gabriel had been out fishing and came to the nursing station with an Arctic Char. *Annette this is for you and your nurse.* Well this is the Inuit culture sharing with those who cannot go hunting and fishing. In the old days when the Inuit lived on the land it was a matter of survival. Once the elders had lost their teeth, they were no longer able to chew the raw meat and would walk off into the ice and snow to die. We studied this scenario in biomedical ethics at University of Victoria. Was this ethically correct to let your grandparents go and die on the ice? The ethical reasoning was yes as this is another person's culture and who are we to make decisions according to white man's rules.

Now I had the task of cooking the fish. Well anyone who knows me well knows that I do not cook. I put some real lemon juice on the flesh and wrapped the fish in tin foil and put it into the oven. Arctic char do not have scales and hence would cook fairly quickly. When it was ready, Paula and I had a very tasty supper. No, I am not taking up cooking on a regular basis.

One day, I was off to bed at 11 o'clock and I could hear this "bang, bang," on the nursing station steps. It was a 6-year-old girl playing golf on the steps. *"Oh could you please go down to the golf area as the nurse is trying to sleep"*. *"Ok"* and off she went. There was a small patch of grass where there was a three-hole golf area. Grass is not a common sight on the tundra. The 24-hour daylight really did not bother me. The Inuit would be out fishing all night and would sleep when they were tired. It was not uncommon to have to get up at 4 am to remove a fishhook from someone and update his or her tetanus immunization.

By the end of August, there is ice forming on the puddles and 24-hour daylight is gradually decreasing. Now you may find this hard to believe that children in a traditional Inuit raw meat eating society would get iron deficient anaemia. Unfortunately, with the advent of television and junk food, the traditional diet in the younger generation has changed. One must be cool and emulate the television adverts and soap opera dramas.

The school had reopened and Gabriel wanted to implement an iron deficiency project at the school. Gabriel had collected a 24-hour dietary recall from each school child and used my haemoglobinometer to measure each child's haemoglobin level (iron level in the red blood cells). Once this data was gathered he would have a base line. Gabriel reviewed the data with me before commencing his nutritional plan as there might be a child who required an iron supplement. Most of the children had low iron and were not eating balanced diets. Children are fond of raisins and peanut butter, which are good sources of dietary iron. Oatmeal and traditional meats are readily available and reasonably priced and also good sources of iron. It takes 120 days for a red blood cell to mature and this is where the iron is stored in the blood. In approximately three months he will repeat the haemoglobin tests and compare his base line data with the results.

In came the doctor from Yellowknife and he asked me up to his suite to apologize for telling me that I had made a ridiculous diagnosis of DIC. All was well. I reminded him that English was not the primary language in this community.

It might be necessary to use less refined but very basic language when obtaining histories from patients. For example, When did you last pass water (urinate/ void) *When did you last pee"?* When was your last period/ menses? *"When did you last bleed"?* The Inuit men prefer their wives to see a lady doctor especially for maternity cases. In fact, the community would prefer that all babies be born in the hamlet. There is such a vast traveling distance to the nearest hospital. The health Board demands that all maternity cases are sent to Yellowknife at 38 weeks gestation. If a child were to die under your care, it would be a fearful event. Having said that, a few days later, two five year olds were brought into the clinic. They had found a bottle of Tylenol on top of the mother's fridge and had taken a chair and climbed up and thinking the Tylenol tablets were candy ate them. Iron tablets and Tylenol are the two worst drugs to overdose on as they damage the liver. I called poison control in Edmonton and first they wanted know what the serum levels were. *"Sorry we do not have an advanced laboratory here".* We were then advised of the dose of charcoal. Getting 5 year olds to swallow this is some fun. The medivac was on its way. Luckily, the fast action of the mother and the charcoal saved the day but the children needed drug levels, which could only be done in a controlled environment.

Time for Paula to go to Spence Bay and Valerie was coming from Cambridge Bay to help me. I was on call Friday night and Valerie on Saturday. What we had forgotten to say to each other was the exact change over time. Cambridge Bay was 9 am and Pelly Bay was 8 am. Thinking that I was off call, I decided to have a bath and dye my hair black. As I sat waiting for the dye to work, the phone rang. No big deal. Valerie is on call. She of course thought that I was on call. After 6 rings, I picked up the receiver. It was the mother of one of the pregnant girl's. *"Quick, Quick, Annette my daughter is sitting on the toilet and the baby's legs are dangling out".* "Ok". *" Send someone up to get me and I'll be there".* I stuck my head under the tap, rinsed my hair, grabbed my black tracksuit and flung it on and put a yellow towel round my neck to catch the drips. Dashed down stairs, shouting out to Valerie, *"get up I am off to a premature breech delivery".* *"I am taking the obstetrical bag you bring the pediatric bag and I'll send someone up for you".* To this day, I can still remember what I was thinking as I sat side saddle on the back of Gabriel's skidoo bumping over the rocks, one hand on the bag the other clutching Gabriel's parka. What would people down south think if they could see me now? I arrive at

Gabriel's sister's house and sent him back for Valerie.

The two grandmothers were in the bathroom and the girl on a blanket on the floor. I started an intravenous as a precaution as this girl had a bad obstetrical history and I might need a vein in a flash. The baby was 23 weeks gestation and the cervix was not fully dilated. I knew that I had to try to maneuver the baby out, as it would be attempting to breath now that the body had already made contact with the air. The shoulders had to be delivered one at a time, then the head. At this stage in development the baby had very under developed lungs. Thank goodness for Maggie Myles textbook, which I had studied during my midwifery training. My examiner for my midwifery finals was Margaret F. Myles, the author of the textbook. As Valerie arrived, I had the head out and was starting to resuscitate the baby. You take over here Valerie; I need to deal with the mother who had a history of haemorrhaging follow her last baby. Both grandmothers were at hand and one was the lay catechist so they baptized the baby and named her after a deceased elder, which is a custom in the Arctic. After half an hour the baby died. Later, when I called the pediatrician in Yellowknife, he said, that there was nothing anyone could have done, as the baby was too small and not compatible with life. I had the mother settled and I left the family to visit together. I went out side for some air and Gabriel said, *Annette do not look so sad you have saved my sister. There was nothing you could do for the baby; it was too small.* This coming from an Inuit man made me feel a bit better. Now it was time to sign the birth certificate, the death certificate and have consent signed for autopsy on the baby. The mother would go to Stanton Hospital in Yellowknife for a complete work up.

The next person to visit the community was the obstetrician. Pierre arrived with his ultra sound machine to assist him in gauging the gestation of the pregnant women. Pierre visited the communities in the Kitikmoet region biannually. This time Pierre was in for two days and we all enjoyed a scrumptious dinner including the fresh vegetable and fruit he brought with him from the south. These interim surprises in the North help to keep one sane in this sometimes very hostile landscape.

The following day a young woman from the community came into the clinic as we were closing. She had a sick baby with her. I examined the infant and noted that the infant had inner ear infection. I gave the infant some Tylenol for the pain and fever and commenced the initial dose of antibiotic. The infant responded well and settled down in a bassinette.

Inner ear infections are very common in the north as the Inuit ear canals are much shorter than Caucasian people. One would imagine this is to prevent the fierce winds for damaging the internal structure of the ears. Meanwhile while I was busy with the infant, Gabriel had been talking to the mother in Inuktitut. He told me that her husband was abusing the woman and that she wanted to go to a safe house with the infant. I was unable to cope with this abusive situation and noted how well Gabriel was managing. So I took him aside and told him that this was too close to a situation that I had recently escaped from myself and I felt that I could not be therapeutic in this case. You are doing well and you speak the woman's first language. Please continue and I will keep an eye on the infant. This arrangement worked well and we found a safe house for the mom and babe. The next day Gabriel would speak with the woman's husband. In the end there was a positive outcome and the family were happily reunited. Gabriel told the husband that should he require further help; he was there for him.

A few days later Sidone, the lay catechist and Gabriel's mother brought her custom adopted 18-month-old daughter to the clinic. She had a very high fever and cried even when she was touched very gently. When I examined the little one, her ankles, knees and elbow joints were red and swollen and she cried when I touched her. Her throat was also red and swollen. I had never seen a case of rheumatic fever, as this was a rare occurrence at this time in medical history. I had studied the subject and one of my very long-standing friends who had fainted on me in school prayers at the age of ten had had this disease. During my nursing training, we also had to learn how to make a rheumatic bed with soft blankets and no sheets. I gave the little one some Tylenol and called Dr Duncan, the child's pediatrician in Edmonton. He was the little girl's cardiologist. He agreed with my diagnosis and that we should start penicillin treatment and that he wished her to be seen in Edmonton. Sending the child to Edmonton was not an easy task as the mother had to hold the child all the way there on the two flights. I had an idea. We could use a padded cross. This type of board was once used to strap a newborn baby to with rhesus negative antibodies in order to perform a blood exchange transfusion. This procedure is no longer used in developed countries as we can detect the Rhesus negative incompatible blood during the pregnancy. I asked one of the Inuit carpenters who worked for the government if he would oblige. He kindly did and on receipt of the newly made board, I padded it with soft cotton wool. Then Sidone could carry the board and refrain from touching the child except to feed and change her. To be innovative does help when working in isolation. One organism that causes Rheumatic heart disease is streptococcus viridians and if someone has this it attacks the heart valves and the kidneys. Once one has had this problem, prophylactic penicillin coverage is required for all dental and any surgical treatment for the rest of the person's life. The child had a reasonably comfortable journey to Edmonton and after Dr Duncan's expert care whilst in hospital, the little one return to the community a healthy and happier child.

It is now November and the moon can be seen in the sky at 2 PM in the afternoon. The day light hours are very short. It is now time to say farewell to my favourite community of Pelly Bay and make a short stop over in Cambridge Bay to say au revoir to my colleagues and meet the new regional doctor who was another Brian.

In my home in Victoria I have my Pelly Bay Artic treasures on display in the entrance hall. A dog team with a man dressed in seal clothing who has a spear in his hand and there is a seal popping it's head through the ice in the distance. The dog team is pulling the Komotik (sled). The diorama sits on cancellous bone of a caribou and the whole thing is carved from the teeth and the jawbone of a caribou. If you hold the carving upside down and look at the configuration of the dogs, you can recognize the shape of the molar teeth cusps. Agnes, an Inuit elder who spoke no English, had designed a very traditional wall hanging of two Inuit girls dressed in their summer parkas, babies in the back cutting up a seal with an ooloo knife. The girls' faces resembled Stone Age people their hair is braided and made from caribou fur. Agnes's wall hanging is on my staircase wall. The Inuit are very ingenious in many things they do.

My contract has concluded and I am off for a short break in Victoria. My next contract will be in Northern British Columbia.

Chapter 8

༈

FORT WARE AND TSAY KEH DENE

AT THE beginning of December 1990, I left Victoria for a two-week contract and flew to Prince George where Bev, the nurse I was relieving, met me. We stayed in a motel on the Hart Highway. I gave Harald's friend Don a call and we went to the Irish pub for a drink. Don is originally from Newfoundland and works in Prince George as a welder at one of the paper mills. Don and Harald met in St Johns, Newfoundland. We had a pleasant evening and on the way back from Tsay Kay Dene I would rendez-vous with Don again and take his two husky dogs for a ramble.

Next morning, Bev and I set out for the Health Canada office in Prince George where we met all the staff. Arlene, the zone director; Margaretann, the zone nursing officer; Gayle, the assistant zone nursing officer and Iain Baird, the environmental Health Officer. Then we all went for lunch and later Bev and I reviewed the programmes and files of McLeod Lake, Fort Ware and Tsay Keh Dene. Bev and I went for a bite to eat and then back to the motel.

Next morning, with all the vaccination material, medications, supplies and 6 metal patient file boxes, we set off for McKenzie duly named after Sir Alexander McKenzie. On the way there, we saw a couple of moose on the highway. *"Oh stop Bev, I have never seen a moose before, as they do not live on Vancouver Island"*. I was quite fascinated by the little beard, one of the distinguishing features of the male moose. On we went up the high-way to the medical services office in McKenzie to meet the clerk, Annette, who was to go with me to the communities. Then Bev took me along with all the paraphernalia to the motel and left to go home to Fraser Lake on her break. My daughter Amanda was living in McKenzie, so we got together on the weekend and explored McKenzie. The main economic base in McKenzie is two pulp and paper mills. On the Monday, Annette and I went to visit McLeod Lake where the Community Health Representative (CHR) toured us around but there were no pressing problems there. McKenzie does have a small hospital so if there are medical problems the CHR can transfer the sick person to the medical clinic or out patient area of the hospital. Bev had all the immunization up to date.

Next Morning, loaded with all the supplies, we took off in our Canadian Government-chartered flight for Tsay Keh Dene. Tsay Keh Dene means the people of the mountains and 377 First Nation People live here. The people of the Tsay Keh Dene belong to the Kasan Nation who originally came across the Bering Straight during the last glaciation and spread from Northern British Columbia into what is now known as the Yukon. In 1968 WAC Bennett, the Premiere of the Government of British Columbia had flooded the lands belonging to the Tsay Keh Dene people around the area of Williston Lake to make one of the largest earth filled hydro dam projects in the world. In return for the flooded lands the people of Tsay Keh Dene had received funding to build new houses, a new clinic and a school, which were currently under construction. We landed on the airstrip at Tsay Keh Dene with all our supplies and the pilot took off. Normally, some one from the community would come with a truck to take us along with our goods and chattels to the clinic, but no one was there and no one turned up. The community health representative (CHR) was out of the village on stress leave leaving us with a communication gap. There was several feet of snow on the ground so we hunted around and found a flat piece of wood and a piece of rope. We tied the rope to the board and loaded our goods onto the board. Annette insisted on acting as the sleigh dog. I helped move us along to the nursing station by pushing the board from behind. Thank goodness Annette had been here many times before as we were situated in the forest. We finally arrived at the clinic and moved ourselves in. The accommodation was extremely basic, but we did have running water and a flush toilet. The sleeping quarters were attached to the clinic. The bed sheets were full of holes from cigarette burn marks and the mattresses looked like something had taken bites out of them. Now I know why we were told to take our -40°Fahrenheit sleeping bags with us. One was for survival, in case of a crash-landing. Secondly, there were frequent power outages and thirdly for comfort. We had something to eat and got ready to hold a clinic. With the CHR out of the village, Annette did the clerical duties and I saw patients. The people found it quite amusing that we both had the same name. I was Annette 2 and my companion was Annette 1. During the clinic, a man who was working in the construction area volunteered to drive us round the new housing area. As there was no one else waiting to see us and it was now 7 pm, we decided to take this opportunity to do a community health exploration which is an important part of a community health nurses job. We put a note up to the clinic door to tell anyone who was looking for us how to find us. It was hard to believe that we were not in a suburb in a downtown Vancouver because the houses, new school and soon to be new clinic were very modern. Another feature not usually found in the wilderness is street lighting. We thanked the man for his tour and now realized why no one had come to pick us up from the airstrip. All able bodied persons with trucks were working on the new building construction sites. It is difficult to ascertain how many houses are actually here with the amount of on going construction.

Next morning, we held a clinic and in the afternoon we did some home visits on the clinic's skidoo. It was fun navigating through the narrow treed paths. Snowshoes would have been useful. We enjoyed visiting the elders and listening to stories of the old days. We were offered tea in every house and it is very offensive to say "no thank you". Next day, all was peaceful including the weather and we had a radio call from our pilot that he would be in for us on the airstrip at around 1200 hours. For our flight to Fort Ware we packed our bags and using our improvised mode of transport to the airstrip set off at a good pace. We got there in good time, which gave us a chance to look at the Spirit houses in the graveyard. This is the only First Nation's community I have ever visited that has graves that look like these and at the time I took my photograph, no one had informed me of what I have written below. As I cannot undo my mistake, I am sorry if I had been disrespectful. Perhaps, I shall look on what I have done as part of my community health knowledge and assessment. On my next visit to this community in the summer of 2004, I took some pictures. Native people were originally cremated. Spirit houses were built as a home for the ashes and sometimes personal effects. Though Natives began burying their dead in the second half of the 19th century these lodges are still built on top of the burial site. Spirit Lodges are respected as the resting-place of the dead and tourists are requested not to visit these areas or take photographs. In my role as a community health nurse, I was responsible to make a community health assessment on which I would base my practice. In light of this knowledge I required to know the history of this type of grave. These and other Yukon First Nation burial sites are sacred places that are now protected under land claims agreements. Markers, spirit houses, and related artifacts and bones cannot be disturbed. Any accidental discovery of such a site, which might be found near old villages, camps and trails, must be reported.

After a short flight to Fort Ware, where the store manager had come to pick up the mail, flown in with us, took us in his truck to the clinic. Fort Ware has a population of 425 Cree people, 68 houses, one school, a church and a co-op store. This is where the Kwadacha Nation, home of the Tsek'ene people, live and is located at approximately 570 km north of Prince George in British Columbia, Canada. The village lies at the confluence of the Fox, the Kwadacha, and Finlay rivers in the Rocky Mountain trench. Information in the Hudson Bay archives in Winnipeg, Manitoba notes that Fort Ware was part of the fur trade for the Hudson Bay Company circa 1929. Inscribed on a plaque in the vestibule of the church in the village of Fort Ware is the following information: In December 1979, the log church in Fort Ware burned to the ground. After fifteen years of holding church services in a converted house, the people of the remote village of Fort Ware, have come together to build a new log church. This church will be a testament to the craftsmanship, cooperation, and resilience of this remote community. The building will serve the varied spiritual and religious needs of the people in Fort Ware.

Following the missionary efforts of the Immaculate Sisters of Mary and the years of residential schooling at Lejac Indian Residential School, the people of Fort Ware became Roman Catholic. Over the years, various people have joined different Christian groups, as well as formed their own private Christian beliefs. This church will be a place for everyone, regardless of sect or creed, to seek spiritual guidance, relief and peace. The logs were peeled and decked, ready for construction in the Spring 2003. The original church bell from the old church was cracked, and a bell was donated from a church in Ocean Falls, B.C. This bell was hauled by truck to Prince George by Father Brian Ballard. It was then transported over 430 kilometers on radio controlled logging roads to Fort

Ware. In the late nineties Father Brian was killed in a floatplane crash. I had the pleasure of meeting him and Sister Elaine later at Takla Lake in the mid 1990s during a visit by the Bishop who was my houseguest. Many isolated communities will miss Farther Brian. *"Mussi Cho"*, thank you, Sister Elaine, who works alongside us and kept us focused on our project.

As it was too late to start a clinic I decided to go to the store and see what it had to offer. As I was about to leave, a patron grabbed the store clerk girl by the throat and I did not wait to find out what the problem was. The nearest detachment of the RCMP operates out of Tsay Keh Dene, which is approximately 70 km south of Fort Ware. The detachment operates with four members and one public servant. I returned to the clinic and checked out our sleeping quarters. Déjà vu. Oh well, we did have our sleeping bags and it was time for some food. We did an evening clinic as I had a great deal of sexually transmitted disease (STD) to deal with in the form of a mini gonorrhea epidemic. One has to trace all the listed persons and treat them and their sexual partners. If the partner was not in the community and lived somewhere else, I had to get hold of the community health nurse or doctor in the area. This task would keep me occupied for a few hours. All prenatals had to be seen and some well baby immunizations required attention. Luckily, there were no emergencies as there had been in the past weeks. A week before our arrival in Fort Ware there had been a man involved in a fight and he was still in hospital in Prince George with gun shot wounds and the other man in the altercation had been killed. Friday rolled around and it was time to fly out and go back to Prince George. Bev would be back after the Christmas break and I was off to drive to Anahim Lake. I would return to Fort Ware and Tsay Keh Dene in July 2004.

Chapter 9

ς

HISTORICAL INFLUENCES ON THE
INDIGENOUS POPULATION

THE FOLLOWING information is contained in the Hudson Bay Company records in Winnipeg Manitoba: in the 1600s, the Hudson Bay Company came to Canada under the Governance of Henry Hudson and the British Government. Many of the Hudson Bay men who had excellent work ethics came from Stromness in the Orkney Islands of Scotland, and this was the last port of call for the sailing ships to take on fresh water. This was the start of the fur trade and sadly, the Aboriginal peoples of North America also suffered for their involvement in the fur trade. The fur trade created competition that led to wars between First Nations peoples. As voyageurs, the French travelers, moved through the continent, they brought with them European diseases such as smallpox. These diseases wiped out as much as 75 percent of First Nations peoples. Adding to war and disease, traditional ways of life were further demolished as Aboriginal peoples turned to new ways of living and alcohol. It is only in recent times that First Nations and Inuit peoples have been able to begin to reclaim their culture and their place. Along with the alcohol and small pox came European education of the Indigenous People.

In 1820, the Anglican presence in Western Canada was established when the Rev. John West who held the first Church England service in the colony and established the Red River Academy encouraging the Indigenous People to raise up their own missionaries and teachers. The growth of the Red River Settlement, north east of present day Winnipeg, led to the creation of the Diocese of Rupert's Land in 1849.

In the book, Many Tender Ties in the Fur Trade by Sylvia Van Kirk she describes in 1884, Kenneth McKenzie an employee of the American Fur Company had a country wife, married but not kirked. The couple had two daughters and in 1897 the church viewed the two 13-year-old girls as ignorant, Indian women in a miserable state almost naked and starving, who required to be taken from their mother and educated in the Church Missionary school, Red River Academy. The two girls were brought up and educated in European fashion and were never permitted to see their mother again. The Canadian Government Department of Indian and Northern Affairs records mention attitudes of the European settlers prevailed until the mid 1960. The Canadian Government promoted this attitude. On reflection, many years later we can see clearly that despite good intentions, this dictatorial thinking has created many problems and almost destroyed a culture of values and traditions. There were many mainstream religious groups involved in the attempt to Europeanize the Indigenous People as well a Federal Government policy.

In the 1960s, First Nations had little control over their own education. Many students were sent to church-run residential schools where they were cut off from their family and community and their language and culture were discouraged. Residential schools caused a conflict for the children between what they learned at home and what they learned at school, making it difficult for them to be reintegrated into their bands after years away from home. The federal government assumed responsibility for educating First Nations people, turned control over to the churches to relieve themselves of the financial burden of operating residential schools. The purpose of the residential schools was to assimilate First Nations people into mainstream Canadian society. The curriculum in the residential schools was supposed to be on par with the provincial public schools, however the quality of education was inferior. Few First nations students graduated from high school, and virtually none went on to post-secondary studies. In 1961 only twelve First Nations students in B.C., of over 20,000 living on reserves (age 15 and over), acquired a University degree. In 1965, 32, 000 First Nations children were still in federal schools and only 417 reached grade nine, that is just over one percent, and only 50 students continued to grade twelve. The first target of the residential schools was to destroy the Indian languages. By the 1960s the Thompson language of the Lytton First Nation was on the verge of extinction. A culture cannot survive without its language. When the language is lost the culture is crippled. At residential schools First Nations children were not allowed to eat their traditional foods, visits from parents were regulated, and they were not allowed to speak to anyone about what went on at the residential school. If the children were caught doing any of the above-mentioned things they would be whipped. Also, in most residential schools the children were inadequately fed while the teachers and administrators of the school ate well. The children usually ate porridge, and if it was not porridge, it was boiled barley or beans with a slice of bread spread with lard. The sexual abuse of First Nations children was prevalent at church-run residential schools. In the 1950s and 1960s a Roman Catholic priest at a residential school near Williams Lake had sexually assaulted thirteen Native boys over seventy-five times. He pled guilty to charges of sexual assault in 1989. In the 1950s and 1960s the federal government adopted a new policy of integrating First Nations students into the regular provincial school system. By the end of the 1960s almost all residential schools were closed or shifted to non-church control. First Nations students' acceptance into the provincial schools depended on the desire of the parents to send the children, and the agreement of the school boards to accept the children. While integration into the provincial school system seemed to be the start of equality concerning First Nations education, it was not so. *In the provincial schools Native children were seated separately from the white students, sometimes even put into a separate classroom, and the Native students had to wear their residential school clothing.* When a First Nations student was expelled or suspended from school he/she was labeled a delinquent under the Juvenile Delinquent Act and he/she became a criminal. However, when a white person was expelled or suspended from school a report was sent to the teacher, the superintendent, and to the school board, and the student was permitted to return to school. The textbooks in the provincial schools portrayed First Nations less favorably than any other ethnic group. They were referred to as savages, primitives, unskilled, aggressive, and hostile. When First Nations were involved in wars it was called a massacre, but when Europeans were involved in wars it was called a battle or fight. As a result of integration absenteeism was high and students began to drop out of school. In the 1960s First Nations people had the highest dropout rate in Canada, and still do today.

In 1967, the National Conference on Indian and Northern Education was held in Saskatoon to examine the problems of the school systems for

Native children. They examined the school system and it's policies, curriculum, teaching methods and textbooks to find out why the school system
failed to provided satisfactory education for Native children. Discussions
were held to address each of these issues and ideas were generated on
how to improve the school system in regards to the education of Native
children.

In 1969 Ray Hall, Regional Superintendent of Education for the Indian
Affairs branch, stated that a young First Nations student "entering the
school system had a 75 percent chance of finishing grade ten and a 50
percent chance of graduating from high school, and the chances of entering or graduating from University are so remote, it is barely worth con-
sidering from a statistical point of view." Of the more than 49,000 First
Nations people in B.C. there were only 25 who attended University. Hall
did not believe that putting First Nations students in the same classroom,
as non-First Nations students would provide a total answer to a situation, which involved complex cultural and economic factors and was the
culmination of hundreds of years of exploitation followed by bumbling
paternalism. One veteran teacher of the time stated "I think it is very
difficult for most teachers, and I'd be one of them, to deal with Indian
children because of the experience which Indians have undergone since
the Europeans came to this continent. He came as a destroyer, physically
through the barrel of a gun, through alcohol and venereal disease and just
straight power." Several First Nations people who attended school in the
1960's stressed that the school system did little to prepare them for entry
into a competitive white society. The school system had fostered, rather
than helped eradicate, a poor self-image. The students saw themselves
dominated by white people in a system, which refused to recognize either
their native language or culture.

On March 15, 1967, Minister of Indian Affairs and Northern
Development, the Hon. Arthur Laing, spelled out the governments seven
point policy with respect to First Nations education in Canada: A complete education for every Indian child for whom the government has responsibility, according to his needs and ability. Close collaboration with
the provinces to provide education for Indian children in provincial
schools, colleges and universities; the transfer of federal schools in reserve communities to public school boards where the Indian community
agrees to this transfer; provincial inspection of Indian schools which remain as federal schools. A fuller participation by Indian parents in school

affairs through consultation between parents, band councils and reserve community schools; the participation of Indian people on the established school boards where Indian children are a significant part of the school population in provincially established school districts. The school curriculum in federal schools is to be that of the province in which the Indian schools are situated. The curricula will be modified only where this is necessary to meet the special needs of the pupils. Residential schools will be used only for those primary school pupils for whom they are an absolute necessity. They will operate under the full control of the Department under regulations established in close consultation with the churches operating them. All federal schools will operate at the provincial standards applicable in their locality. The educational program will be closely coordinated with the Development Directorate of the Branch to ensure that the needs of the rapidly developing community are adequately met. The aim of this policy was to provide effective education to all Indian children of school age and all Indian children of kindergarten age. All Indians who wish to continue their schooling beyond high school as far as their talents, ability and willpower will take them. All adult Indians who wish to improve their educational status.

In 1971 the Education Branch of the Department of Indian Affairs and Northern Development published a study entitled "5000 Little Indians Went to School". The study followed for years in the progress of 5000 First Nations children who began their education in federal schools in 1964. Three major conclusions came about from this study. The earlier the child leaves federal school to enter a provincial school the better are the chances of successful progress in the early grades. The ability in the language of instruction, which means mastery of a second language, for most Indian pupils, is a key factor in success in school. That unless the schools encourage Indian children to study their own language as a curriculum subject, children who reach the high school level and continue their education in various secondary programs might give up their language entirely.

Chief Dan George believed unless a child learns about the forces which shape him: the history of his people, their values customs, and language, he will never really know himself or his potential as a human being. Chief Dan George has an interesting perspective on integrating First Nations children into provincial public schools: "You talk big words of integration in the schools. Does it really exist? Can we talk of integration until there is social integration? Unless there is integration of hearts and minds you have only a physical presence and the walls are as high as the mountain range. Come with me to the playgrounds of an integrated high school. See how level and flat and ugly the black top is but look now it is recess time and the students pour through the doors. Soon over here is a group of white students and see over there near the fence a group of native students and look again the black is no longer level. Mountain ranges are rising, valleys are falling and a great chasm seems to be opening up between the groups. Yours and mine and no one seem capable of crossing over. But wait soon the bell will ring and the students will leave the play yard. Integration has moved in doors. There isn't much room in a classroom to dig chasms there are only little ones for we won't allow big ones at least, not right under our noses. So we will cover it all up with black top cold, black flat and full of ugliness in its sameness.

Michelle Bryant (Indian name) Bil hem'nex. Michelle is from the Lax Kw'Alaams Band, Port Simpson, British Columbia. This was her answer. I know you must be saying tell us what do you want. What do we want? We want first of all to be respected and to feel we are people of worth. We want an equal opportunity to succeed in life, but we cannot succeed on your terms. We cannot raise ourselves on your norms. We need specialized help in education. Specialized help in the formative years and special courses in English. We need guidance counseling and we need equal job opportunities for graduates, otherwise our students will lose courage and ask what is the use of it all.

I am pleased to write that in 1980's, I was at the University of Victoria British Columbia with Chief Dan George's granddaughter, Shaunee. We were in a small study group together. After graduating with her nursing degree, I visited Shaunee in Port Alberni where she administered an intermediate care facility for the elders with all the traditional food, art and other aspects of the Nuu-chah-nulth Nation. I have another friend, Peggy who you will meet later who had a grade eight education. I encouraged her to upgrade her education. This she pursued and she attended University of Victoria and graduated with her degree in Social work

At this time, various churches have made verbal and written apologies to the Indigenous People. The Presbyterian Church in Canada acknowledges with deep humility and sorrow the harm and exploitation imposed on the Aboriginal People of Canada by our church in cooperation with the policies of the government of Canada to assimilate Aboriginal People into the dominant Western European cultures and religions.

In turn the Federal Government of Canada after much legal deliberation have verbally apologized and will financially compensate the victims for their suffering.

Only time will tell of the outcome of all this as the impact of the history has many relationships to the work of the community health nurse. Disease factors such as AIDS and HIV infections, alcoholism, suicide rates and late onset diabetes are much higher in the indigenous population than in the rest of the ethnic groups in Canada. Loss of the cultural ways in hunting and fishing and a diet of natural food and lack of exercise have had an impact on late onset diabetes statistics. Loss of self-respect and cultural ways has added to the alcoholism and suicide rates. The numbers of Indigenous persons in the Canadian correctional system far outweigh the other Ethnic groups.

Chapter 10

༒

ANAHIM LAKE AND THE WEST CHILCOTINS

ON DECEMBER 20, 1990 I flew from Fort Ware to Prince George with all the metal file boxes and medical supplies to put back into the regional Health Canada office in town so that Bev could collect them on her return to work. The assistant zone nursing officer, Gayle met me at the Prince George airport and assisted me with these items. On the way from the airport to the office Gayle mentioned that Margaretann wished to meet with me. At the meeting Margaretann offered me a Government contract, higher salary and more opportunities for professional development than the current subcontracted agency employment. I thanked her and accepted the offer. A formal interview would need to be conducted in Vancouver with the Regional Nursing Officer, Kaye and this would happen at a later date. Margaretann asked me to take the Anahim Lake nursing station truck to the mechanic for a tune up. After completing this task I called Muriel, my supervisor at the agency and told her that I had accepted a Federal Government appointment with Health Canada and I would be faxing in my resignation. Muriel was disappointed and asked me to meet her for dinner the following evening.

The workday over, I called my friend, Don, whom I was staying with and he came and collected me from the office. We enjoyed dinner caught up on our activities and enjoyed a good movie.

In the morning Don was off to work at the Pulp and Paper mill and I took the dogs for a walk. Gayle was to come by around 11 am and collect me and we would go to the medical supply store to pick up purchases for the Anahim Lake Station and the truck from the mechanic.

After work Muriel and I met for dinner and she offered me more salary if I would stay with the agency. I thanked her but declined the offer then I drove back to Don's house.

In the morning, I started out for Anahim Lake and arrived in Williams Lake where I stayed the night. Next morning I started out down Highway 20 past Alexis Creek where I stopped off to meet Corinne and Lynne, the two-community health nurses in this area. They in turn introduced me to Mary, the Red Cross out post Nurse. I would work closely with all three of theses nurses despite the distance in kilometers between us. I passed Redstone reserve, the home of the Alexis Creek Indian Band, where I would spend a good deal of time in the very near future. I passed the store and post office at Chilanko Forks and then the gas station. We are now in ranching and logging country. On down the road to Puntzi Mountain and now there is nothing but gravel to drive on and a small amount of snow. Yes this was highway 20. Several logging trucks passed me loaded with large logs, which were well tied down. A wave came from each driver. I also passed the Beeline courier that would deliver the prescription medications to me on a weekly basis. Lunchtime rolled around and I stopped off at the Graham Inn in Tatla Lake for a meal. I met the owner Bruno, Ed and Helen Schuck and some of the local ranchers. No one was at the West Chilcotin Nursing Station where I would soon be operating. The only other part time person was Roma who was the clerk and she was on holiday. On I went down highway 20, I passed the school and the church then came Kleena Kleen and Nimpo Lake. Finally, I reach Anahim Lake and drove to the Reserve where the clinic is located. Margaret, one of the nurses, took me to my residence and I got settled in. We would meet again at the clinic in the morning.

The next morning I met the staff and had a brief orientation to the outlay of the station. There had been many staffing problems here and the previous male nurse who had been staying in my current residence had committed suicide. On with the work and we started seeing patients. Wednesday was the day the doctor came in from Bella Coola, which was a long way down to the ocean on a very dangerous stretch of road known as The Hill. In the winter time the police would warn people not to go on this stretch of road and some people just did not pay attention. One woman and her young child had recently ignored the warning and had perished in the deep snow and fridged conditions. Over night there had been a severe snowfall so the doctor cancelled the trip. For me this was a little disappointing as the hospital in Bella Coola was where Doreen from the Thomas Crosby had toured me around and I was looking forward to meeting the medical staff again. Christmas and the New Year, 1991, rolled around and we were kept well occupied with many call outs from gunshot and knife wounds to road accidents and sick babies with middle ear infection, lung infections. If the road to Bella Coola were closed then the ambulance would have a four-hour journey to Williams Lake hospital. I was glad to be at work and making my self-useful as I do not enjoy the madness that revolves around this season. Once more staff was available after the holiday season and now it was time for me to go to Tatla Lake. Roma would drive up and collect me now that she was back to work. Roma would also show me all the paper work, files and varying other ins and outs of the community. I would spend two days per week in Redstone with Iyla, the community health representative, from the Alexis Creek Indian Band.

Roma worked part time and was at work on Tuesday Wednesday and Thursday. So on Tuesday Roma drove down from Tatla Lake in the Health Canada truck to collect me. We had a pleasant drive back and despite the wintry conditions the road was well maintained. Tuesday was a day that I would usually spend at Redstone with the Community Health Representative, Iyla. Thursday was the other day I would spend there. Monday, Wednesday and Friday I would spend at Tatla Lake. These were the mail days and when Roma was not in the office it was my job to deal with the mail. Roma handled most of the First Nations medical and surgical travel but in her absence this was my responsibility. The Tatla Lake clinic was quiet when we arrived and there were no phone messages. So I put my belongings in the residence and Roma and I went to the Graham Inn for lunch and then to meet Utah, the postmistress. Then we went to the Trading Post to meet Elizabeth and her husband, Hughie who owned and operated the local grocery store. Then we went back to the clinic to explore the lay of the land and the paper work. I had brought the Narcotic cupboard key with me from the Prince George Office. I had to do a count of the narcotic drugs and file a report. If there were problems I had to notify Margaretann in Prince George and the Royal Canadian Mounted Police (RCMP) in Anahim Lake. The RCMP would have to come down and investigate any irregularities, as the narcotics are part of the Canadian Criminal Code. Luckily, all was in order and I faxed my report to Prince

George. It was time for Roma to go home and I would conclude my work-day and go on call. I am pleased to say that all was peaceful which gave me time to unpack my things and take five.

If the nurse had to go out to an accident or a house call then one would turn on the answering machine and place an appropriate card on the front door indicating where one was. These methods of communication were also used if one went for a walk or was invited out to dinner or went to church. Mobile telephones do not work well in this mountainous region. The truck had a radiophone, which Roma would use to get hold of me.

The next day was fairly peaceful with a few patients in the clinic for medication refills. Thursday rolled around and Roma and I had planned that she would drive me to Redstone so that she could introduce me to Iyla. This was a two-hour drive there and two hours back. Unfortunately, the weather was so bad that the RCMP had warned everyone to stay off the road, which meant Roma would not be in to work today. I called Iyla and she said that she would call me if she required to should any problems crop up. The inclement weather gave me a chance to check on my drugs and supplies and place orders for outdated stock and replenishments. I could fax these into Prince George for approval. Next day the weather had improved slightly and the snow was up to my waist. I received a call from Iyla requesting that I come to the reserve for a psychiatric emergency. Off I set down highway 20 which had been well ploughed. I reached the Redstone clinic and sat down for a cup of tea with the patient and Iyla. I then gave the patient her overdue long acting anti psychotic injection. All being well, Iyla and the patient and I said good-bye and I started to drive to highway 20. Unlike the main road, the reserve road was not ploughed and as luck would have it, I drove into some deep snow and landed in a ditch. I could not open the truck door. I saw a man feeding his horses and I lowered the truck window *"I think I need some help"*. The man answered, *"Are you the new nurse"? "Yes" "Well I am the chief. "Well I guess I don't' choose any old Indian to help me"* and we both laughed. This is not an appropriate remark to make but oddly enough, Irvine and I became the best of friends. He opened up the back of my truck and retrieved my chain, which he hitched to the back of my truck and then to his tractor. Now released from my prison, I thanked Irvine for his help and drove back to Tatla Lake just in time to collect the mail. It was too late to do home visits so I called the patients to check on them and all was well. Give me a call if you need to and I will be out to see you next week.

It was a quiet weekend and Elizabeth and Hughie invited me for diner. Elizabeth had grown up in Indonesia and was of Dutch origin. Her father was a doctor and when the Japanese invaded Indonesia, Elizabeth and her family were imprisoned. She described how the prisoners were fed polished rice and the husks were placed on the other side of the prison fence just out of reach. To prevent Beri Beri, a vitamin B deficiency, her father had the prisoners drink their own urine. Yes this may sound disgusting but it was necessary to preserve ones life and limb.

It was very peaceful in this part of the country and Iyla and I had many an interesting time at Redstone Clinic. Once a month Dr York would come out from Williams Lake to see patients that I could not handle or who required long-term medications renewed. We had an eye clinic, which was extremely well attended and people turned up much sooner that their appointment times so that they could sit around and visit with one another. Soon it would be time for calving and I was invited to come and observe the calves being born at one of the ranches near Tatla Lake. This was an interesting time.

I went to Puntzi Mountain School and the reserve kindergarten to do the school health programs. The elders were involved in teaching the native language to the nursery school and kindergarten children. The French Nuns at a residential school had educated Iyla but she had managed to retain her native language and would speak to the elders in their own tongue. She said to me one day *"why do you think I am always on time"? "It is because the nuns taught me that and that is why I speak English like a French person"*. She laughed One day I tried to make the coffee and it spilt all over the floor. *"That's it"* Iyla said *"you are forbidden from making the coffee"*.

Break up time and the snow was melting and it was very muddy. One day some of the children asked me if I was the nurse who got stuck in the mud. *"No" "I'm the nurse who got stuck in the snow with a four-wheel drive"*. From then on that is what everyone called me.

Many years ago the first settlers introduced tuberculosis to the Native populations. TB is a rather curious disease in that if not properly eradicated by antibiotic therapies it can lie dormant in a person for years and can reactivate to a new infection. The only other disease that behaved in a similar fashion was syphilis. If the acute infectious phase was not treated by antibiotic therapy the disease would lie dormant for years and many years later would reactivate causing general paralyses of the insane. I have seen only one case of this manifestation and that was in the mid 60's in the psychiatric hospital in Glasgow, Scotland. Widespread uses of antibiotic have been in use since the 50's. In the 60's I worked on a TB ward in Aberdeen, Scotland and there were cases where the resurgence of TB occurred in patients who had previously had active TB and had no antibiotics available to them. These people had been treated with rest, fresh air, sunlight and surgical collapse of the lungs. I started the TB survey at the clinic and then the school. The survey revealed many interesting finds and follow up and treatment were instituted.

June rolled around and it was time for a break. My relief arrived by road and Roma drove me to Anahim Lake to catch my flight home. Flying over the Coast Mountains was breath taking with lots of snow covered crags and hollows in the mountainous landscape. While in Victoria I had to go to the Vancouver office for a formal interview for my appointment with Health Canada. I arrived too early at the Sinclair building so I decided to go to the coffee shop. As I came down the marble staircase attired in my business suit, high heels and decked out with a brief case, I heard a voice from the coffee area exclaim, *"oh there's my little Annette"*. It was Margaretann. Now the Sinclair center inhabitants have been introduced to me. After the interview and paperwork I was appointed to the special projects nursing position. This illustrious title did not alter my assignment in Tatla Lake. In fact it only added to my work assignment.

It was time for a trip to Puerto Vallarta, Mexico with my friend Harald from the Crosby. I had bought a time-share and we enjoyed the sea, sun and Mexican ambience.

Back to reality and Tatla Lake. Down at Redstone we had a problem with a woman who had twice been booked for medical travel but could not go as she was consuming alcohol. I met with the patient and told her that she would not get a third chance as this was Government travel policy. So she went to see the Chief. Next time that I was in Redstone, Irvine came down to see me. I explained the travel policy and suggested that the only way I could think of to get round the problem was if Iyla could be put in charge of ensuring sobriety and that the patient complete the purpose of her appointment. I drafted a contract to this effect and all four of us met discussed it and signed this. The end result was satisfactory to all concerned. One day Iyla had an emergency at Redstone so I drove down and attended to this situation and drove back to Tatla Lake. Roma came out of the clinic to greet me and told me that there had been a horse riding accident at Martin Lake up the hill. I'll come with you and help with the paper work. The young man had fallen off his galloping horse. I applied first aid and Roma used the truck's radiophone to call for a chopper from Williams Lake. We often used Mike, the local pilot, but he was away on holiday. The crew arrived and off went the stretcher in the big bird to the hospital in Williams Lake.

Every ten years the adult tetanus immunizations are up dated. Everyone was down at the fish camp at Puntzi Bridge. Off set Iyla and I and had an adventurous day updating the adults' tetanus status. Kokanee salmon was getting smoked by burning other Kokanee salmon. I thought that was a poor use for good food.

Next clinic was fairly quiet and just as well as one of the men who had been hunting up the mountain with his cousins came in and asked me to go up the mountain as one of his cousins had shot himself. The road ambulance was on its way up the mountainside to recover the body and the priest had been notified. There would need to be a coroner's inquest as this was a sudden death. Iyla drove the truck up the mountainside, as there was no road or path. When we reached the place where the men had left the body, the body had gone and all there was to be seen at the spot was a hat and a rifle. Had the vultures been? Then I noticed the bushes moving further on. I got out of the truck and went over to investigate the situation. It was the man who had shot himself. I did not know this man as he had been in prison for some time lived on the street and involved in drug and alcohol abuse. He had gone into the bushes to relieve himself and was in a sorry state. I asked Iyla to radio for the helicopter. Mike could not come as he was out fire fighting so the Williams Lake crew came. I asked the men if they could chop some trees down to make a clearing for the helicopter to land. Then I asked a lady to bring me down my emergency bag. I started two large sized intravenous infusions and hung them from the neighbouring tree branches. The man was muttering something in his own language. His cousin translated this and said that the man wanted to die. The bullet had gone in through his lower jaw and lodged behind his eye causing the eyeball to bulge. The road ambulance arrived and we transported the man to the clearing. As the helicopter landed the man went into cardiac arrest, Cardiopulmonary Resuscitation (CPR) was commenced with no response. We radioed the emergency room physician in Williams Lake who asked us to stop CPR. The body was then taken to Williams Lake and we left for Redstone. The priest had arrived and I left for Tatla Lake to clean my emergency equipment and my self. My friend Mary and her husband Ernie had arrived from Williams Lake. Ernie was a forester in the area. Once I had finished cleaning it was time for dinner. So we went over to the Graham Inn for a meal. The Graham Inn is a house that was built by one of the pioneers in the area and needless to say the name was Graham. Joy Graham a descendant of the pioneer family still lived in the community. Later that evening the chief's daughter phoned to see how I was as the community at Redstone thought that I was alone and wished to let me know they were thinking about me. I thanked the lady for her concern and told her that I had some friends from Williams Lake for company. Next clinic day at Redstone everyone came out of their homes to greet me and thank me for helping one of their community. This type of response from a community makes one realize that ones work is appreciated.

The drive to and from Tatla Lake to Redstone in the summer was quite the dusty experience. Highway 20 at this point in history was a dirt road, which was well used by logging trucks. If I got behind one of the trucks it reminded me of a Sahara desert storms depicted in National Geographic programmmes. We even had prickly pear cactus growing in the area. The dust made visibility impossible and the dust managed to get into the truck even if the windows were sealed. So to save my lungs, I would drive quite a distance behind the offensive dust clouds so that I could see the road ahead past the truck and if all was clear I would daringly put my foot to the gas and zip by. It was fresh air at last. When I finished clinic, I would have to go back to my office in Tatla Lake and make telephone calls all over Canada in response to community health nurses' job applications. I was already doing the work of two community health nurses and now some of the Prince George office's work.

The local gymkhana rolled around and Iyla came to pick me up and we all went up the hill to Martin Lake to enjoy the event. The turn out was marvelous but after all this is ranching country and the blue birds and swallows kept the flies away.

Time to do the preschool health checks, as school was about to reopen for the fall term. The hay harvest was upon us. One day a lady came to the door and asked if I could come to the hay field and help her husband who had been cutting hay and caught his fingers in the threshing machine. It is really much more advantageous for all concerned if the patient comes to the clinic as that is where all the nurse's equipment is. This was no time to direct the traffic. Down in the hay field was the rancher with his three central fingers on his right hand hanging by threads, the tendons. *"Stitch me up please"*. *"Sorry this is a job for a plastic surgeon"*. He was in shock so I told him that I was going to start an (IV) intravenous infusion and give him something for pain. *"No IV"*. *"Sorry your blood pressure is too low and I cannot give you pain medication"*. *"Ok"* *"Can I give you a tetanus shot and bandage your hand to protect it"*? *"Yes. " I will phone for an air medivac"* *"No I will get one of my farm hands to fly me in my own plane"*. *"Ok, when you are ready to leave, I will notify the hospital in Williams Lake and they will send an ambulance out to the airstrip to meet you"*. When I called the emergency room nurse at the hospital she could hardly believe the story. The man was sent hooked up to an I.V. from Williams Lake to Kamloops to get surgery from a plastic surgeon. The out come was that he has full use of all his fingers.

The tree colours of autumn were beautiful. Red leaves signify that a tree has more sugar in the foliage. The red and yellow hues were everywhere. The gentle breeze blew threw the shimmering aspen leaves and made a gentle rustling sound. Winter would soon be upon us and it was time for me to leave Tatla Lake and Redstone for a break in Mazatlan, Mexico with my friend Harald. Iyla did not want me to go so I had to tread carefully and bring in some humour. *"I have to go home as the hunting season would be here and my hair was so thick that the hunters might mistake me for a moose"*. *"I have to get my hair cut"*. Iyla had an answer for that *"I'll braid you hair"*, she said. *"I miss the ocean"*. Iyla had an answer for that too. *"I'll make up a bucket of salt water"*. It was time to go and I would return in 14 years time. My next posting would be the Labrador Coast where I would work for Grenville Regional Health Services. The head quarters for the north end was Goose Bay and my community would be Davis Inlet, an Innu community.

Chapter 11

ᘓ

DAVIS INLET LABRADOR

IN DECEMBER 1991, my next assignment was with Grenfell Regional Health Services. The main headquarters for Newfoundland and Labrador are in St. Anthonys and the Northern head quarters are located in Goose Bay. I would be working in Davis Inlet located in the Northern administrative area. Sir Wilfred Thomason Grenfell, 1865–1940, was an English physician and missionary, famous for his work among Labrador fishermen. After serving as a missionary to fishermen of the North Sea, Dr. Grenfell went to Labrador in 1892 founding Grenfell Regional Health Services. During more than 40 years of service there and in Newfoundland, he built hospitals and nursing stations, established cooperative stores, agricultural centers, schools, libraries, and orphanages, and opened the King George V Seamen's Institute in St. John's, Newfoundland. In 1912, Grenfell cruised annually in the hospital steamer *Strathcona II*, keeping in touch with his centers of missionary work. 1992 would be the centennial celebration.

Since 1867 when the BNA made health and education a provincial and territorial jurisdiction, health care in Canada has been and still is under Provincial and Territorial jurisdiction, apart from that of First Nations and Inuit which is federally operated by Health Canada. When this administrative legislation was adopted Newfoundland and Labrador were still under British legislative jurisdiction entering Canadian Confederation in 1949. Hence, there is a variation in administration. Health Canada administers health care in a different way. The community health nurse in a community does both preventative health care and maintenance of health as well as treating illnesses. In Grenfell Regional Health Service, the Community based nurse does health maintenance and treatment of illness. The preventive or Public Health is carried out by the Public Health Nurse who for the northern coast is located in Makkovic and travels to Hopedale and Davis Inlet on a regular schedule, weather permitting, as do the dentist and medical doctor for the region. The communities on the Labrador coast consist of indigenous people, First Nations, Inuit, Innu, and settlers. Grenfell Regional Health Services includes everyone.

I flew from Victoria to Goose Bay, which was once a large air force base with North Atlantic Treaty Organization (NATO) and had a large hospital. The hospital is very much smaller now and serving the civilian regional base for Goose Bay and the smaller Northern communities. Sheila, The Regional Nursing officer and I went over to the residence to drop off my things and this is where I would spend the night. Then we went over to the cafeteria for lunch and to meet some of the staff. Following lunch I went to the human resources department to complete my paper work and toured the hospital with Josie one of the Staff Nurses. Then I would meet Sheila who would assign my numerical code number for charting. When one signs a legal medical document you also provided your numerical code number. If your signature is illegible then there is a record of your numerical code number kept in the office in Goose Bay and this will iden- tify the signator.

Next morning I flew to Davis Inlet, a community of 500 Innu people. I was supplied with a handout by Grenfell Regional Health Services, which contained the following information about the Innu People of Davis Inlet. *Innu* means "people" or "humans" in the language of Innueimun. The Mushuau Innu "barren land people" were a nomadic group who hunted the George River Caribou in Labrador and northern Quebec for thou- sands of years. In the late 1960s, the Innu completed their settlement on the northeast coast of Labrador in two communities. The communities were Davis Inlet and nearby Sheshatshiu on the main land of Labrador and nearer Goose Bay. Henriksen, a Norwegian anthropologist who lived with the Innu in Davis Inlet at the time of the relocation in 1967 describes the following. The Innu had difficulties adjusting from their traditional nomadic way of life in the mainland to a settled existence on the island. Government handouts, isolation, boredom and lack of jobs led to alco- holism, something that didn't exist prior to the relocation, according to

Henriksen. Their simple wooden framed houses lacked basic amenities such as running water, sewage and electricity. Since the houses couldn't be moved like tents when they get dirty, the community quickly deteriorated into a slum. Katie Rich, the Chief, while I was working in Davis Inlet describes some of the social problems in her community. The problems of addiction, poverty and isolation plaguing the Innu community of Davis Inlet, Labrador, didn't happen overnight. They can be traced back to 1967 when the Innu gave up the remnants of their nomadic culture to settle in half-built houses on the northeast coast of Labrador. In the beginning, the Innu were hopeful about the move. I will describe more of my current finding as I relate my experiences in Davis Inlet. Yes, this is Canada not a third world country that I am describing. At the airport there were many dogs roaming loose and Rabies is an ever-present disease amongst the canine and sometimes the residents of Davis Inlet. Gordie, the janitor came to meet me with his skidoo and Komotik, a sledge box. Along with my luggage, I sat in the Komotik to get to the nurses' residence, where I unloaded my stuff. Then Gordie took me to the clinic. My orientation had begun. The clinic had two nurses, a clerk, a janitor and a Community Health Representative. As Christmas was nearing one of the nurses, Sue, would go out for her break and another nurse would come to work with me. The community had one water tap in the middle of the village where everyone came to fill their buckets. In the winter time, the water from the running tap would freeze as the person was filling their bucket and they would have to knock the ice off the spout to allow the water to continue to flow. The clinic had water and so did the nurses' residence but the water filter would require Gordie to change it three times a week as the filter clogged up with sand. Needless to say there were no bathtubs or washing machines or toilets and nor were there any out houses. The waste material was put into a "honey bucket" and thrown out the nearest exit. Then the dogs came running to salvage anything that they could swallow. I was lucky to be in Davis Inlet in the winter with snow on the ground. The residence had all the basic plumbing and was located 5 minutes walk from the clinic and one kept one's fingers crossed that when one walked to work that it had snowed to cover up the aroma and contents of the honey buckets.

We had one child who had been badly burned when a propane fire had blown up in her face. She had been in Goose Bay for treatment of her injuries to her face and body and had return to the community. She would come to the clinic on a daily basis for a saline bath in our bathtub. She healed well. Unfortunately she is no longer with us as she was burned alive in a house fire in Davis Inlet with 5 younger children on February 14, 1992. Another regular patient was a man who was constantly becoming infected with boils, very common occurrence in this community due to the lack of baths and bathing facilities.

I asked this man one day when he was in to the clinic for intravenous antibiotic therapy, why his community settled here without sufficient running water? His answer was plain and clear. The Church and the Government promised us health and education. Yes, there was a clinic and visiting health professionals came to visit the community and there was free air transportation to the hospital in Goose Bay. There was a primary school in the community but there was little else. The George River Caribou herd was miles away. The trees were so small and thin that one could stretch one hand round the circumference of a tree, not much use for heating a home in the winter. The cod that was once prolific on the Labrador and Newfoundland coast was gone through over fishing. There was no work and most people made hooch from potatoes, sugar and water to cope with this hideous existence. Children would come to the door of the residence begging for food and the gas tank behind our house was a frequent site of entertainment for the younger generation to get high and hide from the realities of life.

At night if we were called out to a patient at the clinic, the Grenfell rule was that we had to call out Gordie to accompany us. One evening I had a call out from a man who came to my front door. He had been punched in the nose and wanted me to check it and he smelt strongly of hooch. Gordie was out of the community so I took the man down to the clinic to examine his nose. He started getting fresh so I told him I was a witch and that at full moon he could see me on my broomstick flying near the moon. Despite his hooch he remembered this and every time he passed me on the road he said you are the witch. He kept calling the residence to ask for the witch and my colleagues would tell him I was out on my broomstick. Another fellow who had a large head wound requiring stitching was of the same thought to get fresh with me. This time his girlfriend was with him so I asked her to please come into the room so that I could get the sewing done. That worked well.

As the Christmas season came closer, Sue went out for her break and Jennifer came in to help me. Jennifer was from Australia and had never spent Christmas in a snow-covered area. Gordie brought us a Christmas tree and it was sad that Jennifer had to see this particular type of tree as an example of her first Christmas tree in Canada because it was so scrawny and lacking pine needles, that is what grows around Davis Inlet.

One night I heard a noise on our three-way radio, which we always had operating between the clinic, our house and Gordie's house. I called Gordie on the radio but he was not trying to reach us. So I thought that it must have been a fluke and went back to sleep. A few hours later I heard the same noise of voices on the three-way radio. I got up and listened into the conversation and deciphered that it was coming from the clinic. So I called Gordie and he came and collected me and we went to the clinic together. Our Skidoos were chained up outside our house for security so I went on Gordie's skidoo. We found four teenagers sitting on the floor in the clinic sniffing the glue from the cement paste that we had been using to retile the floor. Luckily two RCMP officers were in town, as they would only come occasionally from Goose Bay. So we sent for them and after I had thoroughly checked over the four teenagers for any medical problems, the RCMP took care of the teens. Gordie boarded up the window that the teens had broken in through. He then dropped me off at the residence.

One night a teenage boy brought his mother to the clinic in a Komotik. The woman was rather a large built person and it was hard to get her out of the Komotik. She had been drinking heavily but had a broken ankle.

I told the teen that I would have to send his mother to Goose Bay but that we would have to wait until she was sober. How could we achieve this? He said he would just kick over the bucket of hooch and that would do it. The next day I called for the plane and sent his mother to hospital. During the time in the clinic the night before, the young man told me when his mother was sober she was a very nice person but when she was drunk if he so much as open a cupboard to look for food she would crash his head in the cupboard door. This was a smart young fellow and his teachers at the school had wanted him to go on with his education in Goose Bay but the father would not let him. In the end the father relented and let his son go on to further his education in Goose Bay on a scholarship. The father may have been remembering his own school days in the residential school system.

Another interesting person came to see me one evening as a piece of metal from her skidoo had broken off and became lodged in her eye. I knew she would have to go to Goose Bay where they have an electronic magnet but it was dark and we would have to wait for daylight. I washed her eye well with normal saline, salt and water, and put some ointment into her eye with a patch and asked her to leave the patch on overnight and come and see me in the morning. When she came back to the clinic next morning a tiny piece of metal had come off with the ointment onto the eye pad. I sent her out to Goose Bay on the schedule flight to have her eye examined by the slit lamp.

When a medivac plane flew over Davis Inlet, the community would call it the mission plane from the days of the Grenfell the mission.

I had received several phone calls from Irvine the Chief of the Alexis Creek Indian Band at Redstone and he wanted to know why I was in Labrador and not with his community. I told him these were political decisions and he should speak with Arlene, the zone director in Prince George as that was where he could make his wishes known.

Sue had come back into the Community and it was time for me to go to Victoria. The Public Health Nurse was to take a leave of absence for three months and Sheila had asked me if I would relieve the public health nurse of her position for the three months. I agreed and so we signed the contract and I would go for my break and be back in a couple of weeks.

Chapter 12

ᔕ

PUBLIC HEALTH ON THE LABRADOR COAST

I ARRIVED IN Goose Bay mid January and flew to Nain for an orientation. Maureen lived in the community and did the public heath for Nain, which was a much larger community of 1500 people. My residence was a side room in the hospital. A family of Innu had eaten bear meat and had contracted tricenosis. All of the family members had died except from this one young girl who had muscle wasting and she was in a very poor state of health. Tricenosis is found in bear meat and is caused by the trichinellosis. To avoid the disease proper cooking is necessary and the need to cook the meat thoroughly enough to kill the larvae. Freezing at specified temperatures kills Trichinellosis larvae found in pork but not the trichinellosis larvae found in bear meat which is a freeze-resistant species that remains viable after freezing, even for months or even years. Education concerning the risks of eating improperly cooked bear meat had been done in the community. The pertinent information required to prevent trichinellosis, is that consumers need to monitor for an adequate cooking temperature of 71° C and observe the color and texture of the meat during cooking. A change in color from red to dark gray throughout and a change in texture when the muscle fibers are easily separated from each other are indicators that meat has been rendered safe to eat. However, game meats such as bear are very dark, making interpretation of color changes difficult; for these, adequate cooking might be better judged by texture and temperature information. Microwave cooking might result in uneven temperature distributions throughout the meat. Symptoms associated with trichinellosis include fever, swelling of the face, muscle pain, swelling, and weakness. An increased amount of a white blood cell, Eosinophilia, typically is present in cases of trichinellosis, and elevated blood levels of muscle enzymes (e.g., LDH and CPK) are also common. Health care professionals should consider trichinellosis in any ill person with these signs and symptoms and a history of eating bear meat. Not long after I arrived the young girl also died.

Following my orientation, I flew to Makkovik where I would have my central base and fly from there during the week to either Hopedale or Davis Inlet and when necessary stay at my home base to do the public health in Makkovik which included immunizing the dogs and cats against Rabies. Each month I would have to contact the doctor and the dentist to find out who would be where on what date as we had to share the allocated spaces designated for the visiting health care professionals and we could not all be in the one location at the same time.

Zuska was the community nurse in Makkovik and was originally from Czechoslovakia. Next door to the health centre was the Moravian church, which we attended every Sunday. Men sat on one side of the aisle and women sat on the other side. One day the service was called married peoples' day. I said I could not go, as I was divorced. Oh yes, was the answer come along you are our singing nurse. At the married peoples' service there was tea and buns served in the middle of the proceedings. I found it hard to eat a bun and sing as well. The Moravian services never recited the Lord's Prayer, which I found a little strange but each to ones own way of worshiping.

The weather was exceedingly changeable on the Labrador coast. One day I was scheduled to fly from Makkovik to Hopedale, I boarded the plane and we took off. Next thing I know is the pilot is landing in Davis Inlet. *"Oh what are we doing here"? "Well you have a choice you can stay here, go to Nain or back to Goose Bay as we have lost Hopedale in the snowstorm." "OK I can do some work here".* Gordie came to pick me up and off I went to reorganize my plans to implement health care here and not in Hopedale.

I sat down with the Community Health Representative to plan a hearing and speech test for the pre school children. The children do not speak English and there are no Ps and Bs in Innueimun language. As I do not understand the Native tongue all theses tests had to be done by the Community Health Representative. I would organize the immunization lists and have the clerk call in the children and parents. Heights and weights and eye testing were easy.

During the week the skidoo team covering the Labrador coast for the Grenfell Centennial Celebrations arrived and had to spend the night in Davis Inlet. As there were no extra accommodations at our residence and we only had beds for ourselves the three-man team slept on the floor in the living room. Each village that the team visited had to place something in the time capsule so I put in the recipe for hooch and Katie Rich, the Chief, put in a flag of Davis Inlet. In the morning the three-man team who had originally left from Nain were heading for Makkovik where there was a Bed and Breakfast.

At the end of the week, I flew back to Makkovik for my weekend of rest and relaxation. Zuska came to the airport to meet me with the skidoo and off we went for supper at one of the neighbours homes. When we got back to the clinic there was a call on the answering machine for Zuska to call the store. I left Zuska to attend to her work and went off to my quarters to tidy up and do a laundry. Zuska came down to my room and asked if I would go out to a home with her, as she was a little nervous. An 8 year old child from this house had gone to the store owner and reported that her 18 month old sister was tied to a bed and that her grandfather was drunk and was raping the child. I got on the back of Zuska's skidoo and went to the house with her. The grandfather came to the door waving an axe. We are not allowed to enter a house without an invitation so we had to leave. Zuska was scared to call the RCMP in Goose Bay so I called them and was asked to call social services. The RCMP would be in Makkovik in a few days. I called social services but they were not willing to come to the Community. I told the social worker that this would be documented in my report and that I would pass a copy of my report on to the RCMP. This is a sorry state of affairs. The RCMP came in a few days and the children were taken into the care Social Services but first we had to do a medical check for any untoward injuries. The three-man skidoo team had arrived and I had to add something else to the time capsule as I was in this community now. I had a spare Labrador Rabies Commission cap so I put that in the time capsule and Zuska added the Makkovik flag.

It was time to do the animal rabies shots and I donned my Labrador Rabies Commission cap that I had received along with the rabies vaccine from the ministry of agriculture's office and put on with my parka to keep me warm. This task had to be performed outside the clinic door. I would straddle the dog while the owner held the dog's head and I lifted up the loose skin on the back of the neck and placed the needle in this spot. It was easier than immunizing children. The owner would then come and collect their certificates later in the week. Cats were another story and far more difficult than immunizing children. One had to wrap the cat in a blanket making sure the claws were well tucked in and have the owner hold the pet securely and once again the immunization was given into the loose skin behind the neck.

As the public health nurse, this was one of my experiences that I encountered while serving the people of Davis Inlet. It was a bitterly cold February night in 1992 in Davis Inlet. Six children were left unattended while their parents were out drinking at a Valentine's Day dance. The children were huddled around an electric hot plate to stay warm when the curtains caught fire. A huge flame quickly engulfed their ramshackle home killing all six children. The oldest was nine; the youngest was six months. This Valentine's Day tragedy shocked the tiny isolated community. The fire also thrust Davis Inlet and the plight of the Labrador Innu into the national spotlight. Around 11 p.m. neighbours witnessed the house on fire but had no means to help. *"We had no fire trucks or pumps,"* said Sebastian Piwas, *"there wasn't even enough water nearby to fill a bucket"*. People said there were kids in there. But there was nothing to do but watch the building burn. The six children who died in the fire were Wendy, Jeremiah, Daniel, Simon, Mary Jane and Madeline Rich. Their parents, Gregory and Agathe Rich, were charged with abandonment but a judge in Labrador dropped the charges in 1996, ruling that too much time had elapsed before the case was heard. As a result of the fire, the Innu held an internal inquiry, which led to the publication of *Gathering Voices: Finding Strength to Help Our Children*. The report proposed a seven-step long-term plan including a land claim settlement and establishment of a family treatment centre in the community.

Once again I got into the plane to go to Hopedale and this time the weather was favourable. There had been a case of Tuberculosis reported and I had to go and do the contact tracing and follow up. One morning while I was in the midst of this activity preparing the test dose syringes; the clinic aid came in and told me that we were not doing this today. *"Oh what are we doing"*? *"Get on the back of my skidoo and you will find out"*. There, on the ice was a polar bear with a three-year-old cub. The entire community was out on the ice watching the activity as the two bears headed up the hill. The community had never seen a polar bear before as the polar bear follow a route every year and Hopedale was nowhere near the normal passage route. The mother bear kept turning her head in the direction of the crowd and growling. My colleague, an elderly nurse from Ireland called Ann wanted to go and pat the bears. Not if I have anything to do with it as polar bears are the most ferocious of all bears. Ann was the only person on the Labrador coast with a parrot and she had the last housekeeper and cook, which used to be the way things were in Sir Wilfred Grenfell's time. The cook was Doreen who was fantastic at her job. At lunchtime one day, Doreen served me a cod's tongue, which was a great delicacy. I must admit it was nothing to write home about except that as there were no cod left swimming in the waters on the Labrador coast I would probably never have had a chance to try this morsel again. Once again the weather rapidly turned nasty grounding all air travel for six days. I continued my Tuberculosis tracing and screening. On the second day of the whiteout a young boy of about 8 years old was brought in to the clinic to see Ann. He had abdominal pain, which was diagnosed as appendicitis. Ann called Goose Bay to speak to the South African doctor. "Next time that you have an abdominal emergency send them out before the weather comes down". Perhaps one should familiarize them selves with the Labrador climate before making such wild statements! We kept the child for four more days until we could medivac him to Goose Bay and all was well in the long run.

Friday I flew back to Makkovik and was met by Zuska. There was a head injury ready to go to Goose Bay and the pilot was waiting for the doctor to finish her exam. The pilot was getting a little concerned as the weather was unsettled. He told me to tell the doctor that he would like to leave as soon as possible due to the weather and if she needed to take much longer there would no longer be a choice. We would be stuck in Makkovik. Finally, the medivac team took off and landed safely in Goose Bay.

It was time for me to go back to Victoria but before we leave the Labrador coast I will up date the reader on the progress that was made in Davis Inlet after I left. The report dates back to 1996.

Building The New Community of Natuashish. "We are a lost people." That description by an Innu chief, Katie Rich, seemed fitting when a shocking video of six gas-sniffing teens, screaming they wanted to die, was broadcast to the world. The once-nomadic Innu of Labrador have struggled under a haze of isolation, poverty and addiction ever since they settled in Davis Inlet in 1967. The Mushuau Innu have made progress in addressing serious health and safety issues in Davis Inlet.

In February 1993, 18 young solvent abusers and 30 family members were funded by Health Canada to attend Poundmaker, a native run, six month addiction treatment programme in Alberta followed up by a Davis Inlet wilderness programme run by Alberta trained native councellors. To date, Health Canada continues to fund an ongoing addiction treatment and supportive programme operated by trained Innu addiction councellors. By March 1995 the Canadian Government department of Human Resources had funded training for 75 Innu in construction and crafts trades resulting in employment of 8 work crews 5 led by Innu supervisors. Many physical improvements have been made to the community including new houses, extensive renovations to existing houses and new water and sewage systems. Coexisting with the physical changes is the decrease of alcohol and substance abuse. With proper water and sewage disposal systems general health has also improved. There is a new fire truck and 5 Innu have received firefighting training from the provincial fire department.

The RCMP trained Innu police and the provincial court judge involves traditional Innu methods in consultation with the elders when handing down sentences.

The Mushuau Innu have made progress in addressing serious health and safety issues and in 1996 the shantytown of Davis Inlet moved to the new community of Natuashish, and the beginning of a long healing process. Healing for filmmaker Christine Poker who is telling the story of her people. Innu woman's group, healing means bringing the women of Natuashish together and providing support. And for ex-chief Katie Rich, it means looking for political solutions, such as banning drugs, for a better life for her people.

I was ready to catch my flight home, but the weather was not ready to let me go as a storm blew up. When the snow stopped falling, I went for a walk, but the wet snow was so deep and wet that I had to crawl along the top of the snow to go anywhere. If I tried to walk I sunk into the deep snow and went nowhere.

The next morning, I made it out of Makkovik to Goose Bay and was delayed there due to weather. I stayed at the airport and prayed for a plane to St. Johns. Finally my wish came true and I reached St Johns around midnight and had to sleep in the airport there. In the morning the flight took off for Montreal and once again we were delayed by weather. As we waited for our flights an announcement came to clear the airport, as there was a fire in one of the terminals. It was freezing cold out on the street of Montreal as we waited to get back inside. Finally the flight was called and I boarded the plane for Vancouver and Victoria. My journey home took 48 hours instead of 12 hours. I was looking forward to a break in Mazatlan with my friend Harald.

Chapter 13

༄

WOLLASTON LAKE SASKATCHEWAN

IN MAY 1992, after the trip to Mazatlan, Mexico, Harald and I were back in Victoria. I twisted my right ankle, which was very swollen and I had to elevate it and apply ice. We had been planning to purchase a new video recorder at A & B Sound. Harald was not familiar with Victoria and went by taxi, purchased the new equipment and installed it for me. The following day my right ankle was still very swollen and I still could not get my right shoe on. Harald had to fly back to work in Prince Rupert and I had to fly in the opposite direction to Saskatoon. We said farewell and went our separate ways.

Every time that I worked in a different Province or Territory I had to have a provincial nursing licence to work in that specific region. When I reached Saskatoon I took a taxi to my motel and in the morning returned by taxi to the airport. As I was getting wheeled through the airport lounge, we passed some Inuit men who all stood up and shook my hand. These were men from Pelly Bay, my favourite Arctic community. They had been to a Cooperative Store conference in Saskatoon and there was Mike Heart, the owner operator of the coop store in Pelly Bay. Oh what a small world. We said goodbye and I boarded the plane for Prince Albert. On arrival in Prince Albert I took a taxi to the Health Canada office to meet the Regional Nursing Officer, Trish. Trish took one look at my foot and asked me if I had had it x rayed. No I hadn't. So without more ado she took me to the emergency department of the hospital. This expedition revealed that I had a fracture of my right lateral malleolus and I had to have a fiberglass cast applied. Trish told me that Health Canada would house me in the nurses' residence of the hospital until the emergency room physician gave me the all clear to go north. Trish escorted me over to the residence and bought me some groceries. I really felt like a patient. There were a few nursing students staying in the residence so at least I had some company. Trish did all the necessary paper work from my bedroom. Ten days later I was allowed to go north with a walking cast.

Janette was the permanent nurse in Wollaston Lake and she had one relief person working with her, Ann from a nursing agency with no public health background. Janette had to go out on vacation and Ann and I would hold the fort. We had some interesting support people to work with, a community health representative, Margaret, a secretary, Charlene and the janitor Jeff.

Janette went off on vacation and Ann and I got acquainted. At this point in time we had three different types of meningitis immunizations being administered to young children and it was a complex situation and easy to make errors with. The reason for this transition was due to the manufactures ability to supply us with sufficient vaccine. As I was much more acquainted with the public health régime than Ann, I would take on the role of dealing with the schedules. As I had a problem driving the government truck with my cast, I would let Ann do all the driving. The layout of the nursing station was at an angle to the residence and the two areas were joined which meant we did not have to go outside for emergency calls. If I did have to go out or take a bath I had to put a black plastic garbage bag on my foot to protect my cast from moisture.

The population of Wollaston Lake is approximately 800 people, one quarter of whom are members of the Lac La Hache Indian Band. Other smaller numbers are of non-Status Indians and Metis people. The people of this area entered into Treaty # 8 in 1899 with the British Crown who at that time was Queen Victoria.

Every year the members of Treaty # 8 receive a sum of five dollars each from the RCMP as the representative of the Canadian Government. For this event and ceremony the RCMP are dressed in Full Red Serge Uniform and it is a very interesting custom to observe.

Employment is through existing government jobs, transportation, communications, trades and services, construction, mining companies as well as Band employment in the Band office or schools. Approximately 75% of First Nations People rely on traditional methods of hunting, fishing and guiding as a way of living. Community facilities include a co-op grocery store and fuel station, a post office, an air strip, a theatre, a Band office, a Northern Settlement Office, two pool rooms, two community halls, two charter air companies, two schools offering nursery to grade twelve, a health clinic and an RCMP detachment office. An all-weather road, highway 105, facilitates the ties with La Ronge. Although the road terminates on the opposite side of Wollaston Lake, the community is accessible by winter road when the lake is frozen and is reached by barge when it is not. Medical Services are provided by regular doctor visits from La Ronge.

One day Ann received a telephone call from a European man vacationing in the area. His 10-year-old granddaughter had fallen out of the top bunk and hurt her shoulder. I asked Ann if she could manage this call out and she said yes. I went off to my room. Half an hour later Ann had two patients, the little girl with a bruised shoulder and her father who had caught his right hand in the motorboat engine on the way to the clinic. He was in severe shock and his hand was hanging by his tendons. I inserted an intravenous line and then proceeded to call La Ronge hospital for narcotic pain control, which was refused by the doctor on call. As we conversed the lightning storm that was raging at the time cut the phone lines off. I increased the speed of the intravenous infusion to help raise the blood pressure and gave the patient some intravenous pain control medication Demerol or Pethidine as it is commonly called in Europe. I then proceeded to immobilize the area and prepare for transport once the storm was over. I tried the radiophone and it was working again and I called for a medivac plane to come when the weather was suitable. The storm over and the patient went out for plastic surgery and the end result of all this was a full recovery.

One never knows what will happen in the North.

A few nights later we had another problem with a lightning storm, which knocked out all the power in the community including our emergency generator. Three men tried to get the emergency generator up and running but they had no success. I was on call, so I stationed myself with a blanket in the front office beside the front door because if there was an emergency the telephone would not ring nor would the front door bell and I would not hear a knock on the door at the end of the hall. By now the emergency lights had also gone and by luck there was enough twilight to see a little. A young woman came to the door she had fallen off her all terrain three-wheeler, ATV, and rolled down a gravel bank. She was not badly hurt but had a graze with grit in it on her forearm. There was no way I could see the tiny little specks of grit. So I soaked the area in salt and water and asked her to come back in the day light so that I could properly clean the area and make sure it was free of grit.

I had been told to return to Prince Albert to have my ankle reviewed. Our clinic had an X ray machine and an electric saw.

The opportunity came on a weekend in mid June 1992; all was well with the weather and our power. It was time for me to X-ray my leg. I had to take the cast off but I did not want to use the electric saw as I might incur further damage. I took the bread knife and hacked the cast off.

Then I put on my x-ray protective gown and took the x-ray and developed it. I still have this x-ray to this day as a souvenir. The film was great and I have had no further complaints from my right ankle.

The summer games were on and people from all over the neighbouring countryside had come to town. Five o'clock one morning we had a call from the RCMP that a truck with 20 some people in it had toppled into a ditch. Most people on board had run for cover and all had been drinking heavily. RCMP brought five to the clinic. They were from a neighbouring area and wanted to be flown back to Manitoba, which is the next Province. Sorry I said you are in the area of La Ronge hospital and that is where I must send any one for treatment once I have determined what your injuries are. There was only one man who required to go to hospital in La Ronge so I ordered the medivac and he demanded to see the Chief. I sent for the Chief and explained the policy of the nearest hospital and the Chief settled the man down. Off the fellow went to the hospital in La Ronge.

The following week a woman came in with general malaise, generally feeing unwell, symptoms. She had a slight fever and had green coloured urine caused by over excretion of bile from the body and the whites of her eyes were yellow, which is a sign that the liver is malfunctioning. Palpation revealed abdominal tenderness. Others in the family were unwell. I took a blood sample and sent it out to the lab. The blood test (IgM anti-HAV) is required to diagnose HAV, hepatitis A viral, infection. This test detects a specific antibody, called hepatitis A IgM that develops when HAV is present in the body. At this time I was suspecting Hepatitis, inflammation of the liver. Hepatitis A is spread through infected stool and contamination with food and water. In other words what goes into the mouth and through the gut has an effect on the liver which along with the kidneys is the body's filtration system protecting the body from poisonous material but often rendering the filter organs damage. Hand washing is very important. Until it is determined which type of hepatitis was causing the symptoms, dietary means are used with an emphasis on keeping the liver quiet. Fluids and rest and diet are the best treatment and it is essential to make sure that the person drinks a lot of fluids and eats well. Once we had the blood test results we could use immune globulin, a preparation of antibodies that can be given before exposure for short-term protection against hepatitis A and for persons who have already been exposed to hepatitis A virus to assist the body to heal and protect against hepatitis A infection. Back came the results and we had a Hepatitis A out break. Water supply checks and Immune globulin were needed and we had our work cut out for us. That was not all as all prenatal person have a routine Hepatitis B test. Next thing I know we have a positive case of Hepatitis B in our prenatal population. All family members need to be protected as Hepatitis B is spread by blood contact. More public health action was the name of the game and it certainly kept us occupied.

I receive a telephone call from Margaretann who wanted me to apply for a job in her jurisdiction. This was timely. My Contract in Saskatchewan would be up and I missed the coastal environment. The prairies are flat and there are no mountains or ocean. So why not apply. I thanked Margaretann and sent in my application.

At this time the Federal Government was planning to transfer the control of First Nations' Health Care to the First Nations' control. The Eastern Provinces were well underway with this issue and the Prince Albert Region of Northern Saskatchewan was right in the middle of transfer. Not only was Health but also Education was being transferred to First Nations' control.

This would make the jurisdiction of health and education for First Nations the same as the rest of the inhabitants of Canada. I was pleased to be involved in the transfer process and once First Nations had taken over the administration of the health care all personnel employed by Health Canada on the reserves would be looking for new employment either with a Band or in another of Health Canada's jurisdictions. In the Prince Albert Regional Office, Margaret, the assistant zone nursing officer was planning on transferring to British Columbia and Trish, the zone nursing officer, would also transfer there in time and I would meet the two of them in later years in British Columbia.

One day Ann and I received a call via our radio transmitter from a pilot who was flying a sick child from the Arctic region of Mackenzie into Wollaston Lake. This was an unusual situation as Health Canada Staff organized most emergency flights as it involved cost. We both got into the truck and went to the airstrip to meet the plane. There was an eleven-year-old girl escorting a nine-month-old baby. The baby was badly burned and was crying. Someone had spilt boiling tea over her thighs and she did not even have a baby bottle for comfort. We took the baby back to the clinic and gave the baby some sugar water to drink. We also gave the baby some liquid Tylenol and covered the burns with sterile dressings. Then I called La Ronge hospital and explained the situation. The doctor did not wish to accept the patient. So I called Trish and she said send the child out with the pilot to La Ronge and we will cover the cost. Next I received a call from a woman camping out in the bush and she wanted me to medivac her baby as mosquitoes had bitten the baby. I asked her if she had any oatmeal and she had. So I explained that she could use a basin to bathe the baby and add a sprinkling of oatmeal to the baby's bathwater. This will sooth the baby's skin and make the baby happy.

It was time to leave Wollaston Lake and go home for a break to Victoria.

Back in Victoria I had my hair done and I met my friend Daphne at a Belly Dancing show. She was planning on going to Costa Rica in early January and another friend from the museum; Jeff was also going to Costa Rica. The two of them suggested that I go too. We are going to go to a language school to learn Spanish and stay in Costa Rican homes. Why not I said I can work my contract round that. Jeff said he would make the travel arrangements and Daphne and I would meet him in San Jose, Costa Rica. We would make our own arrangements for the Spanish Classes and Home Stays.

Chapter 14

༒

TAKLA LANDING NOT TATLA LAKE

I N SEPTEMBER 1992, I arrived in Prince George and went to discuss the terms of my contract with Margaretann. I asked to have six weeks at work and two weeks out. As I was working in isolation and by myself on 24-hour call 7 days per week it became tiring and the ability to access groceries, a hairdresser and shops was out of the question. When I came home to Victoria from these isolated communities it was a total culture shock. Usually Simone would come to meet me off the plane in Victoria with a bouquet of flowers. Just driving into town was a stress so many cars so many people. If you ever spent time in a small community and then you went to a large city you will know what I mean. Margaretann agreed with my terms and we wrote up a contract. Now it was time for my interview and my board was comprised of Margaretann, Peggy West and Sandra Teegee who were First Nations women from Takla Lake Indian Band. That over with I had a message to call Iyla. So I returned her call and she told me that one of the elders had died at Redstone reserve and the Alexis Creek Band wanted me to come to the funeral. Chief Irvine had given her permission to come and collect me and bring me to the funeral at the Alexis Creek Indian Band's church on the Redstone reserve.

While I was talking on the phone with Iyla the board had made the decision to hire me for Takla Landing and wanted me to start immediately. What a predicament I was in.

I called Iyla and told her not to come and collect me for the funeral as I had been assigned to go to Takla Landing not to Redstone as previously planned. Iyla was not very happy and she said that I was her nurse at Redstone and she was going to talk to Chief Irvine. Then I got a call from Chief Irvine who asked me what white people are running this government. You are our nurse and we want you back at Redstone with the Alexis Creek Indian Band. I said that I was only a pawn in a political chess game and that he should speak to the zone director, Arlene. I have to go where I am assigned I am disappointed that I was not assigned to be your nurse at Redstone.

I met Don for supper at the Coast Hotel where I was staying and we went to the Irish Pub, which is attached to the Coast Hotel. Thank goodness for some sanity. Some very young man was sitting next to me old enough to be my son but he very politely asked me to dance with him. Don told me that I would be taken up for baby snatching.

Time to go to Takla Landing so Margaretann drove me to Fort. St. James where I stayed the night and then went to the airstrip to board my chartered floatplane. The pilot, Clarence, who I got to know well as I would fly in and out to Takla Landing many times over the next couple of years. We flew over the forest-covered countryside and I sat up in the cockpit with my earphones on. Clarence said to me you see all these purple coloured trees well these are trees that are infected with pine beetle. This was 1992 and today in 2007 the pine beetle is far more widespread.

The Government of Canada's investment of $200 million will attempt to combat the mountain pine beetle infestation in British Columbia and assist in efforts to reduce its eastward spread. The Government of Canada is working with the Province of British Columbia to develop a comprehensive, effective, and integrated strategy to fight the outbreak. The Federal Mountain Pine Beetle Programme measures focus on slowing the spread, recovering economic value, and protect communities and forest resources. To achieve these objectives, the programme will initiate activities on federal, provincial and First Nations lands. Programme details and criteria are being developed. The Takla Lake Band had its own logging company so the Pine Beetles' destruction of the forest had an impact on the community's economy.

I landed on the dock and Peggy and Sandra came to meet me and take me up to the clinic where they introduced me to Richard, the Northern Alcohol and Drug Worker, NADAP, and June, the Community Health Representative Lillian Johnny, the janitor, and her husband Anthon. Ken Murray, the community-visiting psychologist was also in Takla at this time. Then the welcoming committee took me over to the Band Office where I met Chief Michael Teegee and some of the band staff. This was a very friendly Community. It was getting late so we said good-bye and June would help me explore more of the community tomorrow.

Takla Lake First Nation has 587 Band Members and the main community is on North Takla Lake Indian Reserve #7 at Takla Landing on the east shore of Takla Lake, which is approximately 130 km north of Burns Lake. The village had a church and a store, which was also the post office. The mail went in and out one day each week. There were only two telephones in this community one at the clinic and one in the Band Office. These phones were courtesy of British Columbia Rail, which had bargained with the Takla Lake Band that if the Band allowed the rail tracks to run though the reserve then the reserve could have two telephone lines. There was also a Band Run School, which went from Kindergarten to grade 6 after that children had to go to Ft. St. James or Prince George for further schooling.

Next day June's mother, Susan Abraham, came to meet me and she was off on the six-hour journey on the logging road to Fort Saint James and then on to Prince George to play Bingo. Later on I would go with June to meet Granny Teegee, Susan's mother and June's Grandmother.

Babine is the language spoken by the elders in Takla Lake, like most native languages in British Columbia is endangered. Throughout the Carrier Nation only a handful of children speak the language with an estimated 500 speakers, a minority of the population, primarily elders, speak it. Babine is a Northern Athabaskan language named after the First Nation Dakelh People, who live in the central interior of British Columbia. The English speaking population named people who spoke the Babine language the Carrier Nation. My name gradually changed from Annette to Anik, which means granny in Babine. Luckily for me June spoke the Babine language and we went out into the community to meet some of the elders.

First we went to meet and had tea with Ester Abraham a relative of June's. Then we went to meet granny Teegee June's other granny. She was a delightful lady with little or no English and her house was spick and span as were most of the houses in this community. We then went up the road to see Joe Bob who lived at the other end of the village. He was a little more infirm but lived by himself and did his own cooking. Joe Bob had a brother Patrick but these two did not get along and Patrick lived in the

Bush. Most of the people in the village had been hunters and trappers in the old days and everyone had their own trap lines. This activity died out when furs were no longer popular.

At the top of the village road lived the Charlies, William and Amelia, who were a delightful couple. Down the road lived William and Hilda George and their daughter Frieda and their granddaughter, Crystal.

What a lovely community. Wednesday was the day the doctor flew in from Vanderhoof and Dr Stuart would soon be landing and when Dr Stuart was out of the community it was Dr Tony who would fly in to do the monthly medical clinic. Doctor's clinic was usually a busy time. After clinic I decided to go and pick Saskatoon berries so I stuck up a note on the door saying I was picking Saskatoons down at the lake. If one wished to get a message to some one you waited for a child to pass by the door and you would ask them to have who ever you wanted to speak to to come to the clinic. The children were very reliable messengers.

On the Thanks Giving weekend Iyla and her daughter Deana Marie drove from Redstone to stay over night with me. Iyla wanted me to come back to Redstone and Tatla Lake but as I explained Arlene would have to be the one to talk to Margaretann. The Nurse that was now coming to Redstone was Ruth. Iyla drove away to go back to Redstone with the tears streaming down her cheeks.

It was time to visit the school and we started with the kindergarten class and here Linda was their teacher and she had 10 children with an elder, Rosalind Johnny, helping the children learn the Babine language. Then we went to the grade 6 class where Stu, Linda's partner was the teacher.

Next visitor to the community was Sheldon, the dental therapist, who lived in Fort St. James. Sheldon would stay for the week and do his dental program and refer any significant work to the dentist from Fort St James who would take care of the person's needs at the next dental visit. Sheldon had worked in the Arctic in Cambridge Bay before Shirley came but we had never actually met although we had a lot of similar experiences in the Northern Communities. Every two weeks, Ken Murray would come in for three days and on each visit he brought me $ 20.00 of Hershey's peanut butter cups.

On Friday's we had to go to the post office to pick up the mail so Friday for me was home visiting in the morning and administration in the afternoon.

Many people were still up at Bear Lake, the summer camping area, but soon they would need to come back to the village, as the winter would soon be here. Some people were getting ready to hunt moose.

Lillian brought me a moose roast after Anthon had been hunting. I thanked Lillian and Anthon for the gift. Later I watched Lillian in the smoke house cure the hide. Once the curing was complete Susan was going to make slippers with the hide.

Father Brian came in with Sister Elaine once a month to do a service but when he was not around William George performed the lay catechist duties. William conducted the service in Babine and Father Brian, in English. The interior of the church was partly First Nation design and partly what the interior of a small church would look like in a rural area. The lectern was wooden and decorated with Moose antlers.

Anthon was busy carving a new totem pole for the exterior of the new recreation hall. The recreational hall would be ready in time for the Christmas season.

House building was still in progress despite the fact that snow was on the ground.

One day I had an emergency call as a wall had fallen on one of the construction workers when he lost his foothold in the mud. This was almost the end of the day and the light was fading. He had a broken leg but I knew that I would have to send him in by road ambulance to the hospital in Ft. St. James as one required one hour of daylight for the helicopter to come to Takla Lake and one hour back to Ft. St James. So I gave the patient some Demerol and I splinted the leg with an air splint and waited for the road ambulance, which would be five to six hours on the logging road.

One of the work crew suggested that he take the patient in the truck to meet the ambulance half way, which would save time. Ok I said but drive carefully as you will cause pain with every jolt. We padded the back of the truck and supported the air splint with blankets and pillows to prevent movement. I called the ambulance dispatch and told them that the red truck was leaving Takla with the patient and would meet the ambulance on the road. Next day the men came back with my blankets and pillow and I asked how things went. They told me that they never did meet the ambulance on the logging road but had to drive the patient all the way to Stuart Lake Hospital as the ambulance had only had summer tires and had rolled down a ravine. "Wonderful", I said, I will have to call the ambulance headquarters, as that is a hazardous situation putting the ambulance crew and the patient at unnecessary risk by using summer tires on a logging road in winter. June will you please fill out the transportation reimbursement forms for the driver, thank you.

The Band elections were due to be held and I was glad that Ken Murray was in the community, as all hell broke loose resulting in 5 medivacs in one day. One situation arising out of the Band elections was when an irate person who had been voting for another person became violent towards an elder who would not support her candidate. She pushed him so hard that elder could no longer walk and had to be transported to the clinic sitting on a kitchen chair in the rear of an open backed truck. Ken became a great tea maker in an attempt to sweeten things up.

Back to normal, it was time for a Health Committee meeting and we discussed the issues of the last week and made some resolutions. It was now time for the general Band meeting. If you are not a Band member you cannot speak and you have to speak through one of the band Members. William George had asked me to speak at the meeting as he had been round the graveyard and had collected statistics that related to deaths and drinking alcohol. I attended the meeting and had to ask June to repeat all I had to say when asked questions. In the end Michael, The Chief, said *Anik just speak.* The end result was that 20 resolutions were made on the subject of Alcohol abuse and these were sent to Ottawa to be part of the Band legislation at Takla.

I had to start the grade 6 Hepatitis B immunization programme. I collected the parental consents and would implement the first dose in the next week to Stu's class, with the second dose just before Christmas holidays. The final dose would be given in the summer time before school breaks up for the holidays.

In mid October, I went out to Vancouver to an AIDS conference. The Human Immunodeficiency Virus (HIV) is the virus that causes Acquired Immunodeficiency Syndrome (AIDS). HIV attacks the immune system, resulting in a chronic, progressive illness and leaving infected people vulnerable to opportunistic infections and cancers. The median time from infection to AIDS diagnosis now exceeds 10 years.

AIDS is fatal. There is no cure. A medical doctor, Dr. Peter who was dying of the disease, ran the conference. I spoke with him over a patient that I had had and received blood splattering all over me while deal with an emergency in the bush. I had not had any protective clothing or gloves available to me. I may even have swallowed some. This would be classified as an occupational health exposure and it would be better to be safe than sorry. He thought that I should have a blood test as six months had elapsed since the encounter. The Antibody tests are also known as ELISA (Enzyme-Linked Immunosorbent Assay) and is the HIV antibody test.

This test shows whether a person has been infected with HIV, the virus that causes AIDS. The test results were negative. After the conference, I went to Victoria for a break then back to Takla. While I was, home June phoned me for some medical advice. So much for breaks!

Back in Takla we had a very heavy snowstorm and the trees were heavy with snow and many branches fell on to the power lines and cut off the electricity to the community. I had recently had my emergency generator maintained but it would not kick in. Three men from the community poured over the machinery but it would not start. When electricity is cut off even the water does not flow except by gravity and when a certain level of emptiness in the water reserve is reached nothing works. I filled the clinic sinks and bathtub in case of an emergency. The community all had wood burning stoves to cook with and keep the house warm but my trailer did not have the luxury of a wood burning stove. The generator at the teachers' housing complex was functioning so Stu and Linda had me come to their house to get warm, sleep and eat. I did my clinic wearing a toque, two pairs of pants, two sweaters and a parka.

Christmas time came and went with much festivity at the Church on Christmas Eve and of course the Band Christmas party where Michael invited me to go with the elders to be served first. I deferred that Chief and council should go first. Away out in the bush, the sky was clear and it was awe inspiring to watch the lit up Christmas trees and stars twinkling in the clear night sky. In the daytime, the Stellar Jays and Whiskey Jacks would perch on the trees around my trailer waiting for a bite to eat. It was tranquil.

Time to go on my break and it was snowing heavily so the plane was cancelled. Ken Murray and I hired Linda Charlie to drive us out to Fort St. James on the logging road. It took us six hours to reach Ft. St. James and we stopped to get gas at the lodge and got stuck in the mud. We all had to get out and push the truck and I fell flat on my face and was absolutely covered in mud. We decided that it would be better to go to Prince George with Linda, as it was safer on the road than in the air. So Linda drove us to the airport in Prince George. Don came and met me as I had some time to wait and we went for a drink.

Then it was off to Victoria and I literally grabbed my suitcase and left for Costa Rica the next day. We had a great time in Costa Rica learning Spanish, enjoying the ambience of the home stay families and traveling all over on the week end in our rental car. Costa Ricans are very friendly people.

When I came back to Victoria, I would ready myself for Dalhousie University in Halifax, Nova Scotia.

Ruth, now working with Iyla on the Redstone reserve and the clinic at Tatla Lake, and I had been selected to go to Dalhousie University in Halifax, Nova Scotia and we were the first two community health nurses to be selected by Health Canada from British Columbia to take the Northern Clinical Nursing Program.

There would be two community health nurses selected from each Province and Territory in Canada with the exception of Newfoundland and the North West Territories as neither jurisdiction was under the auspices of Health Canada. We would have our fees, travel, and lodgings paid for by Health Canada and receive a stipendium. Each month we would travel back to Vancouver to do a month of practical exposure, as we were not licenced to practice Nursing in the expanded role in Nova Scotia. The program would start in February 1993.

Chapter 15

ᖓ

DALHOUSIE UNIVERSITY

IN EARLY February 1993, I met Ruth at the Vancouver airport and we flew to Halifax, Nova Scotia. Winter still prevailed on the east coast of Canada and we took a taxi to the Holiday Inn, which would be our home, while we attended our Northern Clinical Nursing Program at Dalhousie University. Ruth had an adjoining room to my room. Later, I was happy to know that Maurice from Watson Lake, Yukon, was in the room on my other wall and Joanne, also ex Watson Lake was across the hallway. Another person, Grace, from the Yukon Territory had an adjoining room to Joanne. We all met for breakfast in the Holiday Inn dinning room and there was much hilarity. After breakfast, we all walked up the narrow shoveled pathway through the snow to the university campus.

It was great meeting our fellow classmates from across Canada. Unfortunately, we were not there to socialize. We started classes right away. The Northern Clinical Nursing Program was an 18-month course crunched into four months. The subjects included cross cultural nursing, adult medicine, child bearing and women's health and pediatrics. All subjects included theories and concepts, labs and practicals. One phrase I distinctly remember from one of the pediatric instructors was: If you can't *happy up* the child then there is a severe problem.

The food at the Holiday Inn became a little monotonous and we found a delightful Greek run restaurant round the corner from the hotel. I had a glass of wine with my meal, which everyone in the class came to know as house water. Two weekends in a row we had fire drills. As we all lived on the thirteenth floor it was rather a rude awakening at 1.30 am to navigate 12 flights of stairs in order to assemble in the front lobby. The first time the fire bell went off, I banged on the wall to alert Maurice as he was still snoring. So he got up and came down but the second weekend that the fire bell rang Maurice refused to participate.

We managed to explore Halifax and Dartmouth. In the Halifax grave-yard there are headstones of some of the passengers who drowned when the Titanic sank. One weekend Grace, Joanne, Ruth, Karen and myself rented a car to visit Peggy's Cove, and the Annapolis valley. On the way we stopped in Lunenburg, the home of the Blue Nose Schooner, a roman-tic old sailing ship. The countryside is very picturesque and the excur-sions helped keep some balance in our lives from our perpetual tasks of studying. We would spend hours in each other's rooms asking each other questions after we had reviewed the day's notes of the lectures and labs.

After a month, Maurice, Joanne, Grace, Ruth and I flew to Vancouver for a four-week practical experience. The Yukon did not have the nec-essary clinical venue or exposure required to meet the criteria for the course we were enrolled in. At this time in history, the Yukon did not have its own Registration Nursing Body and Joanne, Maurice and Grace all had Nursing Registration Licences for British Columbia.

We met Pauline our clinical coordinator and the Regional Nurse Educator for the Pacific Region who was a fantastically kind and knowl-edgeable person. We all met on the respiratory unit in Burnaby General Hospital where we were assigned to the medical respiratory consultant. Pauline introduced us to the doctor and we started out by learning of the extensive increase in asthma sufferers in the Vancouver area.

The Cherry Blossoms were in full bloom so this just added to the aller-gic respiratory response.

Neurology was my next practical exposure then Obstetric at St Paul's hospital.

I had to take obstetrical histories in the labour ward and this was quite a challenging experience as none of the patients spoke English.

There were three women in the labour ward one spoke Cantonese, one Vietnamese and one Hindi. International Red Cross cards would have come in very handy as I used these in the emergency department in Aberdeen, Scotland when we had Russian and Norwegian fishermen as patients.

My last assignment for this session was at a pediatrician's office in down town Vancouver. I really enjoyed this experience as the pediatrician had worked with the World Health Organization in Geneva. I would see the patient and then the pediatrician would discuss my findings and treatment plan with me. Then I would go back into the clinic room with the pediatrician and implement my plan. This was what we had to do in our own rural practice setting minus the pediatrician. After my practicum, the pediatrician wanted me to come back and work with him full time in the future. Unfortunately, I was not at liberty to do so as we had to go back to Halifax.

Back in Halifax, the four-hour time change was a nuisance as everyone was asleep and we west coasters were wide-awake. In Halifax, it was still winter with snow on the ground, but finally spring sprung and the blossoms were once again visible on the trees. Our education continued and one person was told as she had failed pediatrics and that she had to withdraw from the program. We continued to plod along and one-week end we decided to rent a car and took the ferry to Prince Edward Island. Now there is a bridge link between Nova Scotia and Prince Edward Island. On the ferry crossing, the foghorn sounded throughout the trip, but when we reached Charlotte Town, the sun was shining brilliantly. We stopped for lunch and later had the famous Cow's ice cream. We drove along the red sandy cliffs that decorate the golden sandy shoreline. The mussels on the east coast are blue as opposed to the black mussels on the west coast. We reached Anne of Green Gables house, part of Lucy Maud Montgomery's Cavendish National Historic Site and has become famous around the world as the inspiration for the setting in Lucy Maud Montgomery's classic tale of fiction, Anne of Green Gables. In real life, this farm was the home of David Jr. and Margaret Macneill, cousins of Montgomery's grandfather. Shortly after her death in 1942, the Historic Sites and Monuments Board of Canada recognized Lucy Maud Montgomery as being a person of national historic significance, and a monument and plaque were erected at Green Gables in 1948. Designated in 2005, Lucy Maud Montgomery's Cavendish National Historic Site includes the Site of Lucy Maud Montgomery's Cavendish Home and Green Gables.

We all had our photographs taken beside a life-sized doll of Anne with her red braided hair and her straw hat.

No more time for enjoying ourselves as it was review time for the final exams. One week we had to take a course on a Saturday. It was the

Advanced Trauma Life Support Certificate Course. That week was a killer 6 days straight of cramming.

Exams over we had to fly back to Vancouver to conclude another month of practica.

In Vancouver I was assigned to emergency and labour room at Surrey Memorial Hospital. The journey to Surrey was a long one on the sky train and then by bus. If we had to do anything after dusk we had to take a taxi instead of the public transit system. This was for safety reasons. The next assignment was at the rheumatology center followed by sick children's hospital where my pediatrician from my last practicum took us to see some triplet's in his care.

Vancouver General Hospital emergency department was next and I landed there on the last Wednesday of the month, which was once known as welfare Wednesday. That is when the welfare payments are made, but is now known as heroin Wednesday as the sale and use of heroin escalates.

We were anticipating going back for our convocation in Halifax, but the cost of two more flights was prohibitive and the budget was already stretched. So we all had our graduation celebration and certificates presented to us in Vancouver. Kaye, the Regional Nursing Officer and Pauline presided at this function and one of the professors came out from Dalhousie University. I found out that I was the last Community Health Nurse in Canada to work by my self in an isolated post setting and soon this position would become a two-nurse post. Ruth in Tatla Lake had another nurse working with her, which was a luxury I had not when I was posted there. Celebrations over I had to return to Victoria to collect my gear for Takla Landing. We all bid each other Bonne Chance and split.

Chapter 16

ᄃ

TAKLA LAKE 1993

IN JULY 1993, I landed in Takla Landing. June, the community health representative was out on vacation and the school was also on vacation. Many people from the village were in Bear Lake camping and fishing. One day Sandra brought in her elderly uncle who had been living out in the bush. He was not feeling well and had a fever and blood was readily visible in his urine. I tested the urine sample with my dipstick, but all that it revealed was blood and protein. I examined the urine sample under the microscope, but could not see anything untoward. I started an intravenous infusion as the patient had also been vomiting and was reluctant to drink. I called for a medivac and the helicopter came to the landing strip at my clinic's rear door. The elderly man was hospitalized in Stuart Lake Hospital in Fort St. James and after a week he still did not have a diagnosis and he was sent to Prince George Regional General Hospital for further investigation. After a month and no further forward on a diagnosis, he was sent to St. Paul's Hospital in Vancouver. He was finally diagnosed with Tuberculosis, T.B., of the kidney and moved to the TB in patient ward. After a few weeks on active treatment, he returned to Takla Lake and he would stay in the village this time. Each week he would come to see me so that I could weigh him and supervise his anti TB medication treatment. He did not want to go back to Vancouver as he said that the other patients on the T.B. ward did not speak English and he had been lonely.

One afternoon, a logger brought one of his co-workers into the clinic.

The man had had several major seizures. The man was in his forties and according to his companion had no known history of seizures. This made good sense as anyone having seizures in the logging industry would pose a hazard to themselves and their co-workers. After assessing the patient, I went to the phone to request a medivac. While I was in the process of making the telephone call a bolt of lightning shot though the phone line and I felt the jolt all the way up my right arm. When I related this event to the Medical Services maintenance chief, Horst, he sent me a fax to make sure my fax line was working with a cartoon that read, beam me up Scotty from the Star Trek television series. Luckily, I did not receive any injury from the event as the medivac team might have had two patients not one to take to Ft. St. James. A new history of major seizure activity in a middle aged person with no known head injury could well indicate two things, a brain tumor or alcohol abuse. I had ruled out a stroke, as there were no signs of physical or mental deficits. It was up to the hospital to further investigate the cause. It was alcohol related.

The Saskatoon Berries were ripening and I thought that I could go off and pick and enjoy some. One evening Sandra came in for a visit and we talked until 4 a.m. I finally said that I had to go to bed and offered her the spare bed, which she gladly accepted.

The end of the summer was drawing to a close and I was running out of food. My Government cheque had not arrived so I could not ask anyone to bring me anything from town in Fort St. James or Prince George. I called Margaretann and told her that I had not been paid and could she please investigate this. Meanwhile I received a moose roast from Lillian and Anthon. Peggy brought me three boxes of clothes and June's eldest boys went to catch some Kokanee salmon for me. The next day I found the salmon on my back door step and the fish had roe eggs inside them.

A piece of alder twig had been threaded through the fish and then it had been twisted so that it was like handle, which made it easy to carry the fish. This is a traditional way of keeping the fish together and making it easy to carry the fish home.

Then the environmental health officer, Iain, arrived and he brought me eggs and a chicken from his farm and some raspberry jam his wife had made. Who needs a government pay cheque when you have friends like this? Yes and it is tax-free!

The Federal government pays northern allowance to persons working in isolated communities and this was the jurisdiction of the Treasury

Board. The man conducting the investigation arrived and he wished to take away my allowance. We sat down to a cup of coffee to discuss this. We are 6 hours at the end of a logging road and there is a floatplane when called in. There is no regular transportation in to Takla Landing. I cannot leave the community to go to town for my basic needs, as I am alone here on 24-hour emergency call 7 days per week. He then wished to go to the grocery store and post office. So we walked to the store. Mail comes in once per week weather permitting and you can see the grocery store has pop, cigarettes, candy and cookies. He concluded his investigation and instead of taking my northern allowance from me, he increased it by two categories.

The next patient to come into the clinic was a teenage girl who had a very high fever, a severe headache and she was nauseated. I knew this girl fairly well and she was not her usual bouncy self. I called Dr. Brown in Ft. St. James and told him my thoughts and that I thought I should start intravenous antibiotic therapy immediately as we had a possible case of meningitis. He thoroughly agreed with me. So I called for the medivac and instituted treatment. Once the diagnosis was confirmed by spinal tap, I would have to do contact tracing and file a reportable disease report.

One morning, I heard gunshots and then June arrived at my house. She told me that a man was drunk and was randomly firing his rifle in the community. She thought that we should call for RCMP in Ft. St. James. We called the R.C.M.P. who said they would come up. The man finally fell asleep and the rifle was removed and brought to me. Not having any knowledge of firearms, I asked someone to disarm the rifle. Then I locked the rifle up in my pharmacy and put the bullets in the fridge. Time went by and it was dark outside. I was eating an apple and cutting it with the only sharp knife I had, which was a large carving knife. A knock came to the door and I thought that it was June. I opened the door with the knife still in my hand and pointing upwards. It was the R.C.M.P., not June. Two young fellows who looked frightened and one asked me if I was the nurse as they wished to use my phone. "By all means, please come in". The pair declined and wanted my office phone. Instead of coming through the living room to the office, they chose to walk round the outside of my residence to the front door of the clinic. I explained that I had the rifle and the bullets locked up in separate places and that the man was fast asleep in his house. One policeman called his office and the other sat with me on the clinic steps out side. He thought that I should whisper as someone might hear what I was saying. I told him that there is no one near as everyone lives up the hill in the village and they are all inside their houses. There are no streetlights or street names in the bush. So I pointed in the direction of the man's house. It was a beautiful clear night and the stars were twinkling in the sky. The two RCMP thanked me and took the rifle and bullets and were on their way to see the owner of the firearm.

It was around noon, when Michael came running into the clinic carrying his nephew and Peggy's son Eric. Eric was 12 years old and had been on a hike with the school. He had an unsheathed knife in his backpack and when he lent forward to tie his shoelace, the knife had punctured his lung. We sat him up with pillows supporting his uninjured side and padded the knife blade and handle to prevent further injury.

I gave him some Tylenol to ease the pain and called for the medivac.

The end result was that Eric fully recovered and was back in the community in a week.

Some people in the area had a grudge against the rail tracks going along beside the village and had burned down the trestle bridge. The railway crew had to replace the bridge and was working on the repairs. I decided to take a walk and see what was happening. When I arrived at the site, it was coffee time and the workmen were on a break. They offered me a cup of coffee from an enormous coffee urn, which I gladly accepted and enjoyed a social chat.

Later, June brought an elder to the clinic, who had a history of high blood pressure. The elder had a severe nosebleed. In fact, I have never seen such a severe nose bleed.

Sometimes, this is nature's way of controlling high blood pressure, but if the nosebleed goes on too long there may be dire consequences such as dehydration and shock. Her blood pressure was in the normal range. So I showed June how to pinch the bridge of the nose and I started an intravenous infusion to combat the loss of blood. I sent for the medivac and gave the elder some vitamin K to enhance the body's clotting mechanism. When the elder reached the hospital the nose bleeding was under control and so was the blood pressure. Dr Brown called me and relayed that the elder was very happy with June and I. The elder didn't think that she needed to leave her village and be in hospital. Next time she had a nosebleed she would just see Anik.

On the weekend the dentist, Andrew, and his wife flew in from Ft. St. James in his helicopter. I just opened the clinic and left the two of them to do their work. They brought lunch and we enjoyed the sandwiches and fruit in a social environment.

A gathering was taking place somewhere out side the village and alcohol was flowing freely. There had been an altercation and a man with a gunshot wound to the head arrived at the clinic. His wife and small child had brought him in. It was always best to stay out of the politics and focus on the health care. The injured man's condition was stable, but I should keep him in over night and send him out when it was daylight. As we were in a mountainous region, nothing was permitted to fly at night in this area, a Transport Canada's regulation. Oddly enough I had no choice but to keep all three people, the man, his wife and small child, in the clinic for the night as the rest of the gathering had surrounded the clinic and were armed with loaded rifles. By morning the armed mob had disappeared and all was quiet. The helicopter landed and the injured man was flown to the hospital in Ft. ST. James and his wife and child went home. Politically, I heard no more about the altercation.

Dr Tony came in to do the medical clinic as Dr Stewart was away on vacation in his homeland of South Africa. Lunchtime came and Tony went over to my house for his lunch. When I arrived he was smoking. So he was reprimanded, as Health Canada does not permit smoking on the premises.

The next visitor was Ken and he was also going on holiday and he asked when was it going to be my turn. Oh I will be going in early January. I will be taking some more Spanish classes with my friends Daphne and Jeff in San Jose, Costa Rica. We will have homestay placements and rent a car so that we can travel around on weekends and after the course.

My next visitor was the Bishop, who flew in with Sister Elaine and Father Brian. The priest and nun would stay in the quarters in the church, but the bishop would stay with me. Luckily, I had been educated at The Convent of The Sacred Heart and we had received general instruction once per month from the Revered Mother on correct etiquette. I actually saw very little of the bishop as he was busy with his pastoral duties.

The day I went out on leave all air travel was grounded due to blizzard conditions. Peggy mentioned that she would be driving out with Eric and his young friend who was going home to his mother in Ft. St. James and then she had to pick up a man and then go to Prince George and there was room for me. I told Peggy that I would pay for the gas and mileage.

We set off on the logging road and had to keep stopping as the snow was impeding the windshield wipers from moving. I had to get out frequently to remove the snow so Peggy could see where she was driving. We made it to Ft. St. James and dropped Eric's friend at his house then we went to pick up Peggy's friend and continue our journey to Prince George. We were in luck and drove all the way to Prince George in the wake of a large Safeway lorry. This pulled us along and kept our vision clear. We made it to the hotel and I paid for a room and as I was thirsty I went to the lobby to get a drink. When I arrived back at the room the place was in darkness and the boys were snoring. Peggy called to me; you are over here with me. Thank goodness, I thought. I told Peggy that everyone would be sleeping when I left in the morning to catch my flight so I would leave an envelope with her gas money in it and square the bill for the room. In the morning, I took a taxi to the airport and the weather was beautiful and calm. The snow had stopped over night and all flights were running on time. I landed in Victoria and went home to prepare for the next morning's flight with Daphne to Costa Rica.

Chapter 17

༄

1994: COSTA RICA TO THE ARCTIC CIRCLE

IN JANUARY 1994, I was off to Costa Rica with Daphne. Jeff was already in San Jose and would come and meet us at the airport. We arrived in San Jose and Jeff took us down town on the local bus. From there we would go to the school in San Pedro where we would meet our home stay hosts.

Next morning I took the local bus to the school and bumped in to Daphne walking up the hill. This would be the routine for the next couple of weeks. The three of us rented a car on the weekends and did some exploring and shared all our expenses with the car rental and hotels. After our three weeks of school, we rented another car for our final week in Costa Rica. On the weekend we went to the yacht club at Puntarenas, where we had been the year before and had enjoyed it. The Costa Ricans or Ticos were preparing for their elections. Political Party slogans were everywhere and the traffic was chaotic. The following day we were going up country so I decided to get up early and go for a swim. There was no one in the pool and I wanted to try out the children's slide. Down I went and crashed my left heel on the bottom of the pool. What a blow that was to my ego as I had once been a 10-metre stunt board diver, and my, what a pain I had in my foot. I sculled to the steps and pulled myself up. I could see Daphne having breakfast in the dining room, but she was too far away to hear me calling her. The gardener and his young son were near the pool so I asked if they could find Jeff in his cabin. Jeff arrived and asked if I had sprained my ankle. No I think it is broken and I better have it x-rayed.

"Con permisso – Si"- the gardener and Jeff carried me back to my cabin and helped me to get dry and gave me some clothes to put over my swimsuit. Daphne arrived and we went to the hospital. I had fractured my left heel and had to have a cast applied. We had four days left of our holiday so I thought I could sit in the back of the car with my foot up. We proceeded on our journey and reached Heredia where we stayed the night. I sat in the hotel while Daphne and Jeff went to find me a pair of crutches. The next day we went to Jaco and ate lunch and then on to Tamarindo in Guanacaste Province and spent the night there. Then we traveled on to Liberia for another night and back to Cartago and Alajuela. There were many stairs to navigate and Jeff was great at carrying me up and down.

Once home, I went to the hospital to get a walking cast and was told that I had to be off my foot for two months and off sick for six months. I was also told I might never walk again. I called Margaretann and told her my bad news. The next six months I spent time swimming so as to strengthen my leg muscles and allow my foot to heel. Today I am still walking with the help of supportive high top runners.

I noticed an advert for an industrial occupational nurse for a summer relief position on the Early Warning Radar System. I contacted Frontec in Ottawa and was told that this was a three-week relief position and as the operation was folding that is all the work that there would be. I am interested in the position, I told the personnel officer and I have worked in the Arctic Communities. I have never been to Ottawa so if I come to complete the security screening and paperwork in Ottawa, would I have time to explore the city? Yes was the answer. "The paper work and meet and greet in the office will not take long and we will pay you and put you up in the Lord Elgin hotel in the city center for two days". I accepted the offer.

In June 1994, I was off to Ottawa and to visit Parliament Hill and sail on the Rideau Canal. Two days went by very quickly and soon it was time to board the plane for Iqaluit. The flight started with a champagne breakfast and frankly I have always found that flights north are more friendly and the service is superior.

On arrival in Iqaluit, I booked into the hotel and explored the community. At dinnertime and I had a marvelous meal cooked by a South American Chef and crème caramel for desert.

Next morning, I flew to Hall Beach where I was met by the base commander and taken back to Fox Main Camp. Fox main had 170 men and was a long-range radar station in the process of converting to a short-range system. I was toured through the radar operations area, which I really did not understand.

My responsibility was to cover health from the Arctic Circle, Yukon to the Labrador coast. I had a nice large room and the food was just like being on a cruise ship.

There were chefs from all over the world and as I was the only woman in camp, I was well treated. Every morning we were awakened by the electronic voice of Betty that told us it was 7 o'clock Zulu time, which is the military term for Greenwich Mean Time. We were a three-hour time difference from the rest of the communities in Hall Beach and Cambridge Bay.

The underground city in North Bay, Ontario monitored all telephone calls and this was where the occupational health doctor could be contacted.

There were still a few men working out on the smaller satellite stations round the Arctic, Yukon and Labrador regions, who were busy converting the radar systems from short to long range. We received visits from some of the high-ranking military officers from Canada and south of the border, as this was a joint US /Canadian venture. I was often tempted to sing a song from one of Gilbert and Sullivan's operettas, "I am the Major General", but did not do so out loud.

I spent time talking and listening to the men at coffee breaks and meal times, which helped defray the tension associated with the downsizing of the DEW line. (Distant Early Warning sites) I toured the kitchens doing a food and safety inspection. If I was required to prescribe any medication, it was done on a specially coded system. One morning, I saw some lovely Arctic Foxes hovering outside the kitchen door waiting for some tidbits. They were all white and looked like a family group.

Next I was sent to Cam Main on Cambridge Bay, a main radar station which housed 100 men and about 12 miles from 675 feet high Mount Pelly, representing the highest point on Victoria Island.

The nursing station at Cambridge Bay was just down the road and I wanted to walk down, but I had to be driven by my driver, as I had to be available for any disaster that might transpire. I went to the Nursing Station, but there was no one there I knew so we drove across the road to the Kitikmoet Health Board where Jean worked. I invited Jean and her husband Ron to enjoy a dinner at Cam Main. The base commander had arranged a helicopter fishing trip and I was asked to join the party. We flew into a large lake area and I enjoyed watching the fishing and the lavish picnic.

One day a man with a sore back was unable to get out of bed.

So I asked the base commander to go with me, as I did not think that it was appropriate for me to go alone. I was teased enough already with boxes of Hershey's Kisses and cards placed in my office mail slot. I took it all in good fun.

My three weeks were up and our flight out to Winnipeg was at 2 am. The base commander came to see me off and told me that I had done a great deal to relieve the stress and tension in the camp by just listening and talking to the men because the closure of the DEW Line was foremost in their minds and they would not talk to each other about this subject. I was off to Winnipeg and home to Victoria. My next posting would be Fort St. James.

Chapter 18

ᔑ

FORT: ST. JAMES, TACHE, BINCHE
AND TAKLA LANDING

WHEN I arrived home in Victoria, there was a phone message from Margaretann. I called the Prince George Office and Margaretann wanted me straight away. I gave my self a few days to get organized and flew to Prince George. I signed all the paperwork and stayed over night at the Coast Hotel and Don came and had dinner with me.

Next morning Margaretann and I drove to Fort St. James. We met Donna, the nurse who lived in Fort St. James and went for lunch. After lunch Margaretann and I looked around the community. She told me that I would be all right when the Indians take over, as they love you. Now I can reflect on this statement, which at the time I thought was rather strange. Margaretann had meant the Federal Transfer Program that was under way in the Eastern part of Canada, which gradually handed health and education over to the administration of First Nations from Federal Government control.

The community of Fort St. James (population: 1,927) is situated on Stuart Lake, near the rolling hills of the Nechako Plateau and the southern edge of the Omineca Mountains. In 1793, Sir Alexander MacKenzie was the first European Scots Explorer to come to Fort St. James. Fort St. James was one of B.C.'s earliest European settlements, founded by Simon Fraser in 1806 as a fur trading post in the district of New Caledonia for the North West Company. Today, the Hudson's Bay Company trading post is a National Historic Site, restored to look as it did in the 1890s having the largest group of original wooden buildings representing the fur trade in Canada.

The history of The Hudson's Bay company spans about one hundred and forty six years, starting with the arrival of the fur traders until it closed the original shop in 1952.

Margaretann and I booked into the motel in Fort St. James.

Next day, Margaretann left for Prince George. I spent a few days in Fort St James getting to know the staff and the community. Then we drove down to Tache where I would be based. En route we stopped at Binche to meet Mary, the Community Health Representative. Mary and I would meet later in the week to discuss her community's needs. We arrived in Tache and we met Priscilla, the Community Health Representative. I arranged to meet Priscilla the next morning to discuss the Community health needs. Donna's husband had driven up the road behind us and he would drive Donna back to her clinic on the Nak'azdli reserve in Fort St. James.

I would keep the brand new Green Ford truck and I was to stay in Tache at the clinic, which was not equipped as a residence. Donna had bought a coffee pot and there was a microwave. Just as well I am not a gourmet cook.

Chief Thomas Alexis of the Tl'azt'en Nation describes the communities that I will be responsible for. The word Tl'azt'en translated means "people by the edge of the bay" and is a First Nation that lives in north central British Columbia. We know ourselves as Dakelh ("we travel by water"), the Europeans called us 'Carrier Indians', because we were nomadic. Our language, Dakelh, is part of the Athapaskan language group. Prior to contact, our traditional territory covered a vast area along Stuart Lake running up the Tache River almost to Takla Lake to the north. The Keyoh or land was managed in family units and the family head controlled the hunting, fishing and gathering in his Keyoh. In late 1800's Tl'azt'en began to gather into central communities in response to the fur-trade and the dictates of the Roman Catholic Church.

The present population of Tl'azt'en Nation is around 1300. Approximately 800 people live in one of the communities of Tache, Binche, Dzitl'ainli, or K'uzche.

Tache, the largest of the communities, is situated 65 km north of Fort St. James at the mouth of the Tache River on Stuart Lake. Tache has the main administrative offices, the elementary school, daycare, Head Start, health and RCMP offices. It is our goal to have our culture and language integrated into all aspects of our education from daycare to high school. Over the years we have trained our people to work in our daycare, Head Start and our community-based elementary school. Binche is twenty-five km from Fort St. James at the mouth of the Binche River, which drains into Binche Lake (Pinchi Lake), and then drains into Stuart Lake. The Pinchi Lake Mercury Mine opened in the 1940's, and again in 1970's. Pinche, the biggest of all the communities now is the smallest. Dzitl'ainli is on Leo Creek road along side Trembleur Lake. K'uzche is on the Tache River. At present our elders are working to preserve, digitize and promote our language, stories and cultural practices before theses are lost. Our people still live off the land hunting moose, deer, bear, caribou, mountain goats, and small fur bearing animals. We set nets for salmon, whitefish, trout, kokanee, spring salmon, and Rainbow trout and still go to our campgrounds in the summer time to gather food for winter storage. For countless centuries the fish and the surrounding wildlife have sustained our people's excellent health and well being, including our relatives in Nak'azdli

I spent the night on the very uncomfortable couch, which had metal ends and reminded me of a bench in an airport. In the morning, Priscilla came to speak with me and she went out into the community to try to find me a proper bed but there were no spare beds.

Now that I was stationed in this clinic, the Community thought that they could come to me for emergencies, but unfortunately I was not equipped to perform this task and my duties involved preventative health care.

I went down the logging Road to meet Mary in Binche and discuss the elder care and immunization programs and plan a date to implement some scheduled vaccinations.

On my way back to my clinic home, I met Paul who was giving an environmental health talk in Tache and he came down to my residence for coffee. He was amazed to learn that I was living in the clinic and said that he would let Iain, his boss, know. Next morning I received a telephone call from Iain who informed me that he was going to tell Margaretann that she had until 4 PM that afternoon to provide me with suitable living quarters. Not long after that call, Donna from Fort St. James called and told me that I was to go to Stuart Lake Lodge where a chalet had been booked for me and I was to go there immediately.

I arrived at Stuart Lake Lodge and was greeted by the owners Christl and Gerhard Meier. The resort was similar to a Swiss village and I knew I would be happy here over looking Stuart Lake. I would drive down to Tache and Binche daily to perform my public health duties. One day I was driving down the paved road and a logging truck loaded with logs passed me at a very slow speed. As the two vehicles crossed over from the paved road to sand road, a small stone hit my driver side window and shattered the window covering me in fragments of splintered glass. The glass was all over the front seat, sticking out of my clothing including my turtleneck sweater. I was so taken a back I did not know whether to continue on to Binche or turn round and go back to Fort St. James.

I chose the latter as I could not even get out of the truck. Back at Fort St. James, I drove to Donna's house and pressed the horn until she came out and she came with me to R.C.M.P to report the damage to the Government truck.

We then drove to the glass factory and the men vacuumed me all over so that I could get out of the truck.

While I was staying at Stuart Lake Lodge, Cristl and Gerhard had to go to Nanoose Bay on Vancouver Island, where they were building a new home in preparation for their up coming retirement. They asked me if I would look after the property and Lodge while they went to Vancouver Island. I said I would be delighted and moved into their son, Andres's cabin, who was a master chef in the Four Season's Hotel in Vancouver. Most of the Cabins were rented to RCMP and their families and a few foresters involved in the logging industry, so I would not be troubled with short-term rentals. The cleaning staff would do the maintenance and laundry. I was invited to a superb meal before the Meiers left for their trip. I would still be able to do my public health in Binche and Tache and could answer any problem calls that concerned the Lodge when I was off duty in the evening. During my time at Stuart Lake Lodge, I was busy doing a family research for Jeff who had birth records of one of his distant relatives, a Native Cree Indian from the Star Blanket Band who was born in 1785. In 1803, at York Factory, she married Jeff's English relative from Middlesex. The distant grandfather was a factor with the Hudson Bay Company. I had to research in the archives located in the historical Hudson Bay Fort in Fort St James and in Library books on early Canadian history and it was amazing the information that came to light. I actually managed to link up the missing gaps in the family tree. My next task was to find out if Jeff had a claim to Indian Status.

Historically the Indian Act has changed several times. Lori Moisey, my clerk, in the clinic at the Nak'azdli reserve in Fort St. James assisted me and took me to the Nak'azdli Band representative in charge of Band memberships. We successfully traced the legal historical links.

Donna went off on holiday and I centralized my work area in the Nak'azdli reserve clinic. Nak'azdli means, "when arrows were flying", as there was once a great battle at the mouth of the river between Native groups. The village is located on Necoslie Indian Reserve No. 1, adjacent to Fort St. James. There is some dispersed housing on Indian Reserve. No 1A. Nak'azdli First Nation services 16 reserves totaling 1,458 hectares. There is the clinic, a gymnasium, a band office, a kindergarten school, and a garage and a craft store.

Much of the economic activities revolve around forestry, arts and crafts, some trapping, and a house construction business. Nak'azdli Band is also one of three partners in Sustut Holdings Ltd. Revenues are also generated from leasing 12 lakeshore lots and a trucking company.

Lori was happy to have me working there and we all enjoyed our time until one day there was a report of a 6-year-old boy with meningitis in the community. It was a Monday morning and I received the call from the hospital. I had to start contact tracing and that was a challenging task as the child had been at a large family picnic when he became sick. I called Margaretann as I required authorization to have overtime to do the necessary work and that included week ends.

My next problem was a few weeks later when one of the nearby reserve's Community Health Representative came to see me and told me that a man who was HIV positive was having unprotected sex with some of the Native women in her community. The man was not informing his sex partners that he was infected with HIV.

It was necessary for me to inform the RCMP of this man's sexual activities and have RCMP contact him as this type of behaviour is against the law.

I then had to go to the reserve with the community health representative to meet the women who had had unprotected sex with the HIV infected man and council them and take blood for an ELSA blood test. Once the results were available, I would have to return to do the post-test results and counselling.

I had received a telephone call from the Arctic and they asked me to open a traditional birthing unit in Taloyoak, Spence Bay. I told them that I could come in November and they could send me the paper work and I would sign it and fax it back.

Donna came back from her holiday and I went into Takla Landing to relieve the couple who were now working in Takla Landing. The wife was the person who had been dismissed from the Dalhousie University Program and was no longer working as a Nurse Practitioner. Her Husband was the Community Health Nurse.

There was a mousetrap in my bedroom and I am not partial to these creatures. I went through to the clinic and found most of the bandages had been nibbled. Hanta virus was in British Columbia and there had been three deaths from this infection, which is spread by Deer Mice, the vector, in the saliva, droppings and urine and can be inhaled from any dust or source contaminated by the deposits of those mice. To clean infected areas use half strength bleach and wear a mask covering your nose and mouth. Mice carcasses should be burned.

I decided that I was not going to sleep in the bedroom but instead I would sleep on the couch in the sitting room with a hammer in my hand. Sure as fate, around 2 am I woke up to see a rather large mouse with large ears in the kitchen area. I had deliberately left the light on in the kitchen just in case of unwelcome visitors.

I banged on the floor with my hammer and the deer mouse went back down the heating vent. Out with the bleach bottle and down the vents went the solution. After that I had no more four legged night or daytime visitors. In the morning, I would bleach the entire kitchen area. In a couple of days, Sheldon was coming in to do his dental therapy with the school-aged children. I was still sleeping out on the couch, as I still didn't feel comfortable in my bedroom. Around 1 am, there was a knock at the door; it was a woman. She had been drinking and someone had hit her on the head and she wanted me to look at her injury. We went through to the clinic and I examined her. There was nothing but a graze and her vital signs were satisfactory as far as I could detect with alcohol on board. I cleaned the graze and put on a light dressing and asked that she come back to the clinic in the morning and I would reexamine her level of consciousness. Off she went home with her friend. I completed my documentation and went to secure the front door and collect my keys from my desk but my clinic door keys were missing. Oh dear, I had better put a wooden chair under the front door handle. So if some one comes in, the chair will fall down and I would hear the noise. I went back to my trailer and watched out the window for a short while, but I could see nothing unusual.

I slept until it was time to get up for work and when I went through to the clinic, my pharmacy door was wide open but no sign of my keys. The chair was still as I had left it, the back of the chair sitting under the handle of the front. I went through to waken Sheldon who had heard nothing and could not believe that we had been broken into. Once the band office was open, I informed the Chief and he said call the R.C.M.P. in Fort St. James. There were pills scattered all over the snow outside the clinic and many of the elders' medications and T. B drugs were what had been taken. I called Margaretann and gave her the information and that I had lost all the clinic keys. She said to call Horst in Vancouver and get one of the maintenance staff to come in to replace the locks. In the evening, I had a call from RCMP in Prince George to tell me that they had located the culprit and that she wished to apologize. My response to the culprit was that she should be ashamed for taking the elders' medication and thanked her for her apology. Next day the maintenance man came in to change the lock on all the clinic doors. I gave him my bedroom and told him he was doing a mouse proof check of the area, as I was scared to use the room. He gave it the all clear and I felt that now it was safe to return to my own quarters once he left.

One day a 30 year old man came to the clinic. He complained of a sore chest, coughing and a fever. I examined him and prescribed a course of antibiotic for his infection. Half an hour later, he telephoned me and told me, Anik I am not feeling any better. I asked him how many pills had he had from his prescription bottle and he told me none. Well, I am sorry the pills need to be swallowed at the prescribed intervals, as I do not have a magic wand. This is often the case when antibiotic are prescribed and if one works with indigenous people the nurse must be aware of this thinking which stems from the days of the shaman. Shaman still exists though you do not hear very much said about these medicine people.

I received notification that there had been iron filings found in a certain lot number of the supply of Amoxil, which was an antibiotic that was commonly used especially in the winter. All drugs on the formulary that the community health nurse is allowed to prescribe come from Ottawa and it takes two to three months from the order date until the supplies arrive on site. I checked the lot numbers for my Amoxil supply and all but 30 capsules that I had in stock were of the recall number. 30 capsules would be sufficient to cover only one prescription and it was now October. I sent Margaretann a fax and asked permission to request a replacement order for my supply of Amoxil from the pharmacist in Fort St. James. The chief Medical officer for Health Canada in Vancouver could write a prescription for the pharmacist in Fort St. James. I would receive the order from Peggy who was going into town on business and that way they would be brought safely back to me and my supply would be back to its quota. I called the pharmacist with the plan, which was duly executed. It was time to go back to Fort St. James for my last week there. On my last evening, Christl had made dinner for me and during dinner I had a visitor. It was Lori Moisey with a beautiful pair of traditional beaded slippers that her Grandmother had hand crafted for me. Many tears were shed. I do not like goodbyes.

Chapter 19

⌇

TALOYOAK NUNAVUT

THE INUIT name Taloyoak describes a large stone blind that was formerly used by hunters to herd caribou for the kill. Taloyoak is west of the Boothia Peninsula, at the heart of the Northwest Passage. Formerly known as Spence Bay, the area has a long history of exploration, including the famed John Ross expeditions in the 1830s' that resulted in the pinpointing of the Magnetic North Pole. Later that century, between the years of 1848 and 1860, American and British ships came to the area in search of the legendary Franklin Expedition. The population is mainly Inuit and is around 900. There is an RCMP detachment, pool, a post office, two Churches, an Anglican Church and a Roman Catholic Church, a Hunters and Trappers Organization, which perform rescue duties amongst other activities, two stores, the Northern and the Coop stores, mainly for groceries.

Boothia Inn is Inuit owned and operated by the Lyall family who were originally from Scotland in the 1800's but have long since integrated into the Inuit community of Taloyoak. The Hotel, which like many other so called hotels in the Arctic settlements more closely resembles a hostel style of accommodation but does have a restaurant attached. There is a day care center, the Netsilik School that has children from Kindergarten up to grade 12 and a branch of Arctic College. There is a recreation center with a pool, an arena and a women's center. The hamlet council offices where the mayor and council administer the hamlet's business. There is the community-based craft manufacturing center of Spence Bay, where packing dolls are made. The dolls are dressed in a duffel amautiit, where the doll carries the baby doll. There are stuffed animal such as Arctic Foxes and Ookpik are also made in the craft center and these industries contribute to the community's economy. I have several animals from Taloyoak in my home in Victoria. One is an Ookpik, Owl, and the other is an Arctic Fox in a white winter fur coat.

Transportation to Taloyoak is by First Air, which operates flights to Taloyoak, via Yellowknife with refueling stops in Gjoa Haven and Cambridge Bay. In the summer time there is an annual barge that brings in dry goods and construction material. Taloyoak's present attractions are primarily its landscape, history, and fish and wildlife resources. Artists, carvers and artisans are prolific in the area.

When I landed in Taloyoak in November 1994, it was wintertime and 24-hour darkness was upon us. The Inuit are used to this total darkness in the wintertime and 24 hour daylight in the summer time. The population does not keep office hours and sleep comes when one is tired. The school, stores and church services follow white man's schedule as does the clinic hours of operation. I did not realize how much this darkness would affect me. I had never been in Taloyoak before so I did not know what the neighbourhood looked like in daylight. I met the clinic staff; Marianne from England was the other nurse who lived in the health centre and Karen who lived with her husband and family in the neighbourhood. Annie, my clerk interpreter was married to Alec Buchan. Mary, the housekeeper made delicious bannock and Roger, the community health representative. One evening Marianne invited me for supper and after we had eaten she told me that she was having her nap. "I do this every day in the dark days". I found out that I was doing the same thing especially on a weekend when we were on call. I would get up and look for the sun knowing full well I would not see it, but we live in hope. Then two hours later, it was naptime, this went on all day. Many non-Inuit southerners become very depressed in the dark days. One night, I was fast asleep and I woke with a jolt as I thought I had slept in and was late for work. I threw on my clothes and then I looked at the clock. It was 2 am and the light of full moon was streaming in my bedroom window. That is how light and dark affected one can become in the dark days.

In the first week of December, Marianne had to go to Pelly Bay for a meeting not long after I arrived in Taloyoak. The staff all went home after the clinic was over and I was alone on call in the health center. The phone rang, a woman yelled down the phone "come quick to house # 30. My son has hung himself". "I asked if someone had cut him down and was anyone doing CPR."

"Yes" to both questions. It was 40°C below outside with a wind-chill factor making it approximately minus 70°C. When it is that cold, it takes a vehicle that is plugged in but not in a garage 15 minutes to warm up. Our truck was outside; we did not have a garage. I called Karen's house her husband answered the phone, Karen had not got home yet. "Please tell her that I need her help". I then called Roger's house, he was not home either, and I asked his wife to tell him that I need him at the clinic. Then I called Annie and she said she would find them and come in to the clinic. I had no idea where house 30 was and needed Roger and Annie's know how on the community. I went outside and started the truck. Roger came and went straight to the map to look for house 30. Roger had grown up in Taloyoak and he did not know where this house was because no one gives house number as the hamlet is small enough that everyone knows who lives in which house. Karen and Annie arrived and by this time the metal on the truck was no longer brittle and the truck was drivable. We arrived at the house and found that the RCMP were there ahead of us. The 13-year-old Inuit boy was lifeless and had been so for some time as his skin colour was gray and he was cool to touch. We attempted CPR and then took the boy to the clinic where all our equipment is centralized. We put him on to our monitors and used the cardiac shock paddles and intravenous resuscitation drugs without success. We then called the physician for the region who was in Coppermine and he told us to stop CPR.

The family was very upset; luckily the local catechist was present and took charge. The mother begged me to keep on trying to bring the teenage boy back to life and I had to tell her that "God had called him" and there was nothing I could do. Everyone including the health center staff and the police were crying. I sent all the staff and police upstairs to have coffee whilst I stayed and dealt with the body and then the family could take him and perform the indigenous rituals.

Next day I asked the mayor and the local member of the Legislative Assembly, John Ningark, to speak to the Minister of Health so that we could get some grief councelling support in the form of art therapy for the children in the school that the teenage boy had attended. Artistic expression is far more beneficial for this type of population than the talking type of counseling. An immediate response from the Minister of Health in Yellowknife provided two art therapists in the community school helping both the children and parents.

Soon it would be Christmas and it was time to hold the Elders' Christmas Party and the Children's party with Santa Claus and our staff Party. Father Joseph had arrived to spend Christmas and the Christmas service with us. All the carols were sung in Inuktitut and the written words were in syllabics. As I knew all of them by heart I just sung the carols in English. We all enjoyed Christmas Day and played some fun games after our turkey dinner accompanied by plum pudding.

I went out in the dark to the Northern Store which had lights round the building and as I walked with my head down in the blowing snow, I heard a broad Buchan accent calling out my name It was Alec Buchan, Annie's husband. What a surprise to hear my homeland accent in this desolate winter storm.

One day some of the men in the community decided to build us an Igloo and give us a treat.

The doorway is built low to keep the howling gales out and the interior temperature was quite warm. The housekeeper, Mary, baked us bannock and took us out to an igloo that had been built for us. We crawled inside and sat on caribou hide on the narrow snow shelf that went round the walls of the igloo. We had a Coleman stove to make tea on and a Coleman lamp for light. It was 2 pm in the afternoon and the full moon was in the sky. This is afternoon tea "lunatic fashion". It was great fun.

We received a call from the Hunters and Trappers association that a man was out on the land and had had an accident. He had gone over a bump in the ice and fallen off his skidoo. Yes this is all happening in the dark of 24-hour darkness. It took 3 days for the rescuers to find this man and bring him back to the clinic. The 25-year-old healthy man was wearing polar bear fur pants and I did not want to damage these. So I asked his wife if she would cut them off her husband so that I could properly examine his injuries. She carefully cut along the seam of the polar bear fur trousers and revealed two parts of the young man's thighbone, the femur, poking through his underwear. This young man required to be hospitalized in the nearest orthopedic hospital, in Edmonton. I called for a medivac, which would take several hours to reach Taloyoak. Pain control was already established and next I had to splint the area in preparation for the flight. Once the patient was settled, I had to make arrangements with the designated receiving hospital in Edmonton. This was the University Hospital, but for some very odd reason I could not get an answer on the telephone. So I called the Royal Alexander Hospital and spoke to the orthopedic Specialist and arranged for the patient to go to the Royal Alex. The medivac arrived and took off for Edmonton. The medivac team landed in Edmonton and transferred their patient for his orthopedic surgery to the Royal Alex hospital. All went smoothly and we settled down for some sleep. Next morning, I received a call from Yellowknife Health Authority complaining that I had sent my young man with the broken leg to the wrong hospital in Edmonton. Our receiving area for patients from the Arctic Communities was the University of Alberta Hospital not the Royal Alexander Hospital. My response was that unfortunately, the University Hospital did not answer the telephone and as the patient was in need of emergency care, I had no other administrative choice.

When the sun finally peeked over the horizon on 15 January, every one at the clinic rushed to the window to have a fast glance, as it was only visible for a few seconds.

A child brought in her traditional bone game to show me. The hollow bone is covered with the inside of a toilet roll and decorated with modern material and held up with a pencil. This was a modern adaptation of the older culture when this hollow piece of bone would have had a piece of animal sinew threaded threw it and not a piece of twisted material. Things change over time, which sometimes is rather sad.

The birthing project was well underway and included much input from the elders especially the traditional midwives. Soon it would be time to open up the project and I was ready to go for a break in Victoria. The sun had peeked over the horizon several times and it would not be long before it was 24-hour daylight again.

Annie and Alec would take a trip to Victoria and we would go out Killer whale, Orca, watching

After my break I was coming back to the Arctic Circle to the western side this time to work in Sachs Harbour, a small community, on Banks Island off the coast from Inuvik.

Chapter 20

SACHS: HARBOUR OR IKHUAK

IN FEBRUARY 1995 I flew to Inuvik in the western Arctic and took a taxi to the hospital. The Regional Nursing Officer showed me round the health care facility where I met June whom I had known from Cambridge Bay and Julie a midwife in Goose Bay. "What a small world".

The Inuit in the Western Arctic call themselves "Inuvialuit" or real human being. European infectious diseases shattered the traditional culture of the Inuvialuit in the late 19th century, before it could be described in writing in any great detail. What we do know has been pieced together from traditional oral histories, archaeological research, and the writings of the various 19th-century explorers, fur traders, and missionaries who visited the Western Arctic. Unlike most places where Inuvialuit live today, Inuuvik (now spelled Inuvik) was not a traditional Inuvialuit settlement. The Federal Government built it in the 1950s to relocate people from Aklavik and eventually many Inuvialuit moved to Inuvik for work, schooling, access to hospital and other services.

Next morning, I flew to Sachs Harbour and was met by the Community Health Nurse, Mary, who was going out the next day on holiday. She showed me round and introduced me to the Community Health Representative, Sheila and the Secretary, Margaret Carpenter. The surname Carpenter is the most prevalent name in Sachs Harbour dating back to when Fred Carpenter built the first cabin at Sachs in the late 1930s establishing a store and trading posting in 1958. Predating the store an RCMP post was established in 1950 and a weather station in 1955.

Sachs Harbour or Ikhuak is the most northerly community in the new Northwest Territories and only permanent settlement on Banks Island with a population of 114 persons.

One of the first explorer ships HMS Investigator, landed at Baring Island in 1851 now known as Sachs Harbour or Ikhuak.

In 1966, the whole of Banks Island was registered as a group trapping area in which only members of the Sachs Harbour Hunters' and Trappers' Association had the right to trap. In 1967, as part of a centennial project, a cairn incorporating several parts of the engines of the schooner, *Mary Sachs,* was erected on the hillside above the town, commemorating the founding of Sachs Harbour.

On the weekend I explored the fascinating wild life arctic willow Ptarmigan feeding in the low creeping willow, flocks of lesser snow geese flying overhead and listening to raven with the many variety of calls. Not surprisingly there are two federal migration sanctuaries here where 43 different bird species visit the area annually. I saw many musk oxen on Banks Island, which is the home to the highest concentration of musk oxen on earth. Disappointingly I did not see any of the endangered Parry caribou, barren ground caribou or any polar bear, only polar bear skins hanging on a fence to dry.

I was happy in Sachs Harbour and we had a lovely retirement feast, when the postmistress and her husband, the school janitor, both retired. It was catered to by the man who drove the water truck and to my surprise, he was an ex master chef from the Empress Hotel in Victoria, British Columbia. The tables were beautifully decorated with apples carved into animals, birds and fish. Some fortunate American hunters happened to be in the community at the time were also invited.

It was fun going out to visit the elders on my skidoo and one day I went to visit the mother of Rosemary Kuptana, president of the Inuit Broadcasting Corporation. The elder had made some lovely wolf mittens and a musk ox. So I bought both of these items. The mittens kept me very cozy while I was riding around on my skidoo. This was a very peaceful community and Margaret, my secretary, told me that she had a brother who was a general surgeon on Vancouver Island.

Just before I arrived in Sachs Harbour, two people had died from ingesting anti freeze, which they thought was alcohol. The time flew past and before I knew it, it was time to go back to Victoria. Mary was about to get married to the owner of the local grocery store and I was asked to come back in two weeks so she could go to her home in the East of Canada to get married.

There had been many American polar bear hunters in the community paying the Hunters and Trappers Association guides up to $16,000 per guided tour. The tour had to be done using dog teams and camping out on the tundra. The use of Skidoos was not permitted. There were many polar bear skins hanging out to dry.

I walked slowly out to the airstrip and two planes had arrived. One was the mail plane and the other was the passenger plane to Inuvik. As I waited in the wooden shack, I was horrified at the conversation from the American Hunters. The conversation was gross and sounded like bar room talk and similar to the one that got away, when you hear fishermen bragging, but this was even more sanguineous. I really did not wish to fly on the same plane with these men. So I ventured to ask the staff at the airstrip if I might travel in the mail plane, but unfortunately passengers are not permitted to fly on that plane. The dead polar bear trophies were loaded on to the plane along with the skins, which no doubt would become a polar bear rug.

Peter Esau, the mayor of Sachs Harbour, was going on the same flight all the way to Edmonton. He told me that he would look after me and he did just that all the way to Edmonton.

In two weeks I was back in the community for another month, which was enjoyable and uneventful.

I was to go to Arctic Red River or Tsiigèhtchic, which was normally not served by a Community Health Nurse as the ice bridge links the community to the Dempster Highway in the winter and the ferry service links the community to the Dempster Highway in the summer. There is only a Community Health Nurse there at break up and freeze up of the Arctic Red River and the Mackenzie River. The Arctic Red River is the name of a tributary to the Mackenzie River in the Northwest Territories. It was also the name of a community at the confluence of two rivers and is now officially called Tsiigèhtchic. The Dempster Highway crosses the Mackenzie at this point forming a road link to the facilities in Inuvik.

Chapter 21

ɔ

ARCTIC RED RIVER TSIIGÈHTCHIC

I RECEIVE A telephone call in the middle of April 1995 and was asked to come to Inuvik as soon as I could as break up had started very early this year. I told the Regional Nursing Officer that I would need two days to get organized and if she would go ahead and book my flight. I arrived in Edmonton and stayed the night at The Nisku Inn. Next day, I arrived in Inuvik and was met by my friend, June, who took me to the Health Office and I signed my contract. June had arranged a ride down to Arctic Red River Settlement with The RCMP. The Chief, Grace Blake, and Alestine Andre, an anthropologist, who was a graduate from the University of Victoria, met me at the band office. Alestine's father had been the Chief before Chief Blake. This was a small community, which was normally connected to the main Dempster Highway by the ice bridge or by the Ferry when the ice has gone. The Ferry is a free ride and is the oldest operating ferry in Canada.

Missionaries of the Roman Catholic Church first came to Arctic Red River in 1868. The church was built in 1921. Traders from the Northern Trading Company and the Hudson's Bay Company established rival posts at the river mouth in the 1890's and early 1900's. The RCMP had a detachment here for much of the 20th century. Albert Johnson, the "Mad Trapper of Rat River", killed one constable from the Arctic Red River detachment. Now Tsiigèhtchic is a native community where ancient traditions of living with the land blend with modern lifestyles.

I had days when I could just listen to the elders when I went on home visiting. The elders would tell me about their lives before the white settlers. This was an interesting community and very peaceful which gave me time to explore and enjoy the ambience. Alestine explained to me about what she had found in the midden down on the rivers edge, which proved that there had been an active settlement here for many years. Alestine Andre's archaeological digs at the mouth of the river indicate that the Gwich'in utilized this excellent fishing eddy centuries before Alexander Mackenzie first gazed up the river in 1789. Elders in the community tell stories of the annual migration up the Arctic Red. Families and bands of people would head upstream once the river level dropped in the late summer. They were heading for the foot of the North Mackenzie Mountains, over 280 km from the mouth of the river. When the flow of the river became too swift for easy upstream travel, they would head overland.

Winter camps were established on fishing lakes at the base of the front ranges of the mountains. The people survived the winter by hunting caribou and Dall's sheep and by catching fish through the ice on the lakes. In the spring, they would return to their summer camp at the mouth of the river. Some of the old portage trails can still be found. If one listens carefully, the voices of these travelers can still be heard echoing off the black shale cliffs.

Arctic Red River *(Tsiigèhnjik)* is a designated Canadian Historical Heritage site. The village of Tsiigètchic had been build 10 meteres up from the river for a very good reason. I was privileged to have witnessed an entire week of break up along with the entire community of Tsiigèhtchic as we watched the Arctic Red River break up. It started with a loud bang, which sounded like a dynamite explosion away up the river. Then down rolled all shapes and sizes of ice, cylindrical, square, round and oblong. Along with the large blocks of ice came trees and mud. What an awesome sight it was. The Elders told me that this was the earliest that they could remember the Arctic Red River breaking up. Then there was another loud boom and it was the turn of the mighty Mackenzie River to go through the same scenario and then the most amazing thing happens. Of all the outstanding natural features of the river, its hydrology is the most fascinating. During the ice break-up in May, the level of the Arctic Red can rise 10 metres above winter levels. The Arctic Red typically clears itself of ice before the Mackenzie. When the Mackenzie River's ice breaks, it too will rise 10 metres or more. Mackenzie River ice is then pushed up river along the smaller Arctic Red. In years of high water, Mackenzie River ice can be pushed 70 kilometres up the Arctic Red. The flowing ice leaves scars on riverbank trees, 5 metres above the river surface. The villagers of Tsiigèhtchic have built their homes up above the flood level of the river.

Dale Clark told me to come down to the river mouth and watch him cutting off ice from the ice blocks, which the population used to make tea. His wife Rose then invited me to try the ice water tea and taste the difference from the tea that is made from the tap water. Another day, Dale asked me to come and see the Loche fish that he had caught, which lives in the frozen river all winter. Rose then invited me to their home to sample the Loche fish, a type of white fish, which was delicious.

The Arctic Red River is considered a navigable waterway in the Gwich'in Land Claim agreement. This means that visitors are free to utilize the river as a transportation corridor. Some restriction to access and use are placed on Gwich'in private lands and the visitor is advised to contact the Gwich'in Tribal Council in Fort McPherson or in Tsiigehtchic before travelling on the Arctic Red.

Accommodation and Services: The community of Tsiigèhtchic offers the visitor a store, automotive services and gas. While there is no formal camping area, visitors are welcome to camp on the flats near the ferry landing. Inuvik is 120 kilometres north of Tsiigehtchic along the Dempster Highway. Inuvik offers a full range of accommodations, restaurants, campgrounds, specialty shops and air charter operators and outfitters.

During my time in the village of Tsiigètchic I had little demand on my time in the way of emergency health care and found time to visit the school and meet with the children and the teachers and attend to preventive health such as updating immunization schedules in the population.

Now that the ferry was up and running, I had no need to be in the community as the inhabitants of Tsiigèhnjik had access to health care in Inuvik at the hospital or at the Nursing Station in Fort McPherson, where I would work in 1998. I had had a call from Charlotte at Health Canada in the South Mainland Zone Office and I was to go to Klemtu on the West Coast of British Columbia for the summer.

I was asked by Chief Grace Blake to go to the band office for a meeting at 5 PM. When I arrived the whole community was there and what a feast awaited us all. I was presented with a thank you card signed by everyone and a beautiful pair of ornate slippers and was told I had to perform a dance. So I did a type of Highland fling to the delight of all. Rose and Dale gave me a happy face and a thank you note. I was only in the community for a month, but I really felt that I was part of the family. Grace gave me a ride up to the airport in Inuvik and off I set for Victoria.

Chapter 22

ᕗ

KLEMTU

J UNE 1995, I flew to Bella Bella and then by float plane to Klemtu where Bruce Robinson, Community Health Representative and Marge Starr, Clinic Secretary met me at the dock and we drove up to the trailer, where I would be staying. We opened up the clinic and I got to work. Having visited Klemtu on the Thomas Crosby and met Bruce and Marge before nothing much had changed and I knew most of the community. There was a brand new Nurse, Rhea, working with me, so this made life more interesting. Colleen Robinson was another Community Health Representative who worked part time and would relieve Bruce when he went on holiday. Everyone called me "Miss Netty".

Klemtu is a small village on Swindle Island, situated on the province's spectacularly beautiful central coast. Two distinct tribal organizations live here: the Kitasoo who were originally from Kitasu Bay and the Xai'xais of Kynoc Inlet. The Kitasoo/Xai'xais people are the only permanent residents within the traditional territories of the First Nation. The Kitasoo/Xai'xais Nation has a total membership of approximately 460 people. The population of the community has doubled in the past two decades and is expected to continue growing at that same rate.

For years, the mainstay of the Kitasoo/Xai'xais economy was commercial and food fishing. However, the severe downturn in fish stocks has had a devastating impact on employment levels. To cope with this situation, the Kitasoo/Xai'xais felt it was imperative to diversify their economy. They are now turning to tourism, aquaculture and forestry to create employment opportunities for their people. They wish to preserve their cultural values as well. Their task is to balance the ecological values with the rights and needs of their community for economic health, including lasting job creation. The Sea Eagle and the Killer whale are two of the Klemu's Family Emblems. While deeply aware of the need to provide jobs for their people, the Kitasoo/Xai'xais also embrace the important environmental, cultural and ecological values of their territory. They want to protect fish and wildlife habitats, including that of the Kermode White Bear, flora, and all the other important elements of a forest's ecosystem. Up to 10% of the black bear species in the Kitasoo territory have white coats, even amongst the same family. Under the Kitasoo Land Use Plan, a total of 40% or the region is preserved and available to sustain the White Kermode Bear as well as other fish and wildlife values. During my stay in Klemtu, I was fortunate to see a Spirit Bear and the traditional belief in Klemtu is that the Kermode is a reminder of the last Ice age, which occurred around 12 thousand years ago. The Spirit Bear or White Kermode Bear (Ursus Americanus Kermodei) lives in this remote habitat and is a sub species of Black Bear. The mother and father bear may be black in colour but the cub may be white. Every tenth bear is white.

I went off to visit some of the elders. Heber and his sister Marianne were home and Marianne was in the process of crocheting a tablecloth for a wedding. Murray and Sandra were to be married in a few weeks and soon it would be time for the wedding shower. The crocheted tablecloth was used initially at a wedding ceremony as an altar cover and then after the ceremony the cloth was given to the newlywed couple.

The Revered Willie Robinson, who I had met at breakfast on the Thomas Crosby in 1989, would perform the wedding ceremony. Saturday, we all tripped to the wedding shower with food galore and lots of laughter. Rhea and I joined Marge and Bruce and the entire community for this fun celebration. The following weekend it was the wedding. There were great celebrations and a wonderful feast.

This is one thing I really remember about this community; they really knew how to serve up wonderful food. Unfortunately, we were very busy in the later evening.

Rhea and I were both busy with a medivac, which we could not send out by air to the hospital in Bella Bella due to the fact that the clouds were right down on the ocean. It was a patient with a serious overdose of Tylenol and we had to enlist the services of the Canadian Coast Guard ship, Sir Wilfred Laurier. I was not aware that one had to accompany the patient on this search and rescue ship, but the Search and Rescue Technicians (SAR Tech.) did not have training in intravenous therapy at this point in history. When the ship arrived at Klemtu, I transported the patient in the ambulance down to the dock and found out that we had to send an escort to operate the intravenous equipment. I called Rhea and asked her if she wished to go with the patient or remain in the community. She was new to this type of nursing, but she was also terrified of the ocean. She wished me to go with the patient. Off I went to Bella Bella, where I delivered the patient to the R.W. Large Hospital where I worked in 1989.

The captain decided to anchor in Bella Bella for the night. The officers' lounge was cleared for me, as there was no cabin available for me to use. In the morning the cook made a wonderful meal and loads of fresh fruit. One misses fruit and vegetable in isolated areas. The other thing that was not readily available in Klemtu was fresh milk and it was expensive. I am not too fond of milk so this was not an issue for me.

Back in Klemtu I called Rhea and all was peaceful so I thought that I would catch some shuteye. Not long after that though, Rhea called me. She had another patient in the clinic, this time the person had taken an overdose of iron pills. This may not sound ominous, but unfortunately, Tylenol and Iron medications are the most potent common legal drugs to overdose on. Off I went to the clinic and helped Rhea. I had to send for the Sir William Laurier again as the weather was not suitable for flying. Off I went with the patient to the hospital in Bella Bella. This time, the ship brought me straight back to Klemtu and I had a good night's sleep and was ready for work the next day.

There was a new baby in the community and it was definitely not thriving despite good mothering. It was the doctor's clinic day and Dr. Smith arrived with an entourage of visitors from Bella Bella. This plane was chartered and paid for by the Federal Government and if the doctor's clinic found patients that require to go to the Bella Bella Hospital for treatment then these patients would fly back with the Doctor. This charter was not a sight seeing exhibition. I did not say anything at this time, but would definitely be letting Charlotte know about this. Dr. Smith saw the baby who was not thriving at the clinic and indicated that no intervention was required and there was no need to carry on weighing the baby. I spoke with the mum and asked her to come and see me the next day. I suspected that the baby had a milk allergy, but to deal with this situation, the baby needed to go to hospital and Soya milk provided. We had none in Klemtu. When the clinic was over, I had two telephone calls to make.

One was to Charlotte about the charter flight, patient transportation and the baby and the other was to my Pediatrician mentor from the Dalhousie Program in Vancouver. Charlotte would speak with the medical clinic in Bella Bella and I called my pediatrician mentor at his home in Vancouver. He said to send the baby down to children's hospital in Vancouver under his care. I called the baby's mum and told her what was happening and we would see if we could get her on a flight tomorrow. Off went mother and babe in the morning and in a week they were both back in Klemtu with Soya Milk. I sent the mother to see the social worker so that she could get a supply of Soya milk. We would continue to monitor the babe, which proved beneficial as the babe grew well. My mentor let me know that yes indeed the babe had an allergy to milk.

One Saturday Morning, Rhea and I went with Bruce and Marge to have breakfast at the Band operated café. After the meal we could hardly move and I needed a siesta. Yes Klemtu knows how to feed you.

I received a call from Rhea. She was having difficulty with a man who had hammered a nail through his middle finger, which was attached to a 6-foot long wooden building plank. I came down to the building site and asked one of the men to cut the plank at either end so that we could bring the man up to the clinic. The ambulance arrived and everyone except for Rhea and I got into the ambulance, which took off for the clinic. Rhea and I were left to walk. When we arrived at the clinic the patient and his companions were let inside. I got out the zylocaine to ring block the finger and in a few minutes the man's finger was frozen and I removed the nail. "Now can you manage? I asked Rhea. He needs a tetanus booster and coverage of an antibiotic. Bone injuries are very prone to infections and of course a dressing. "Thank you", said Rhea and off I went.

When a girl reaches puberty, she is secluded for a few days and is not permitted to eat drink or wash. Other women who have gone though a similar purification ceremony attend her. More than that I do not know as it is a sacred ritual and I was lucky that Marge trusted me enough to tell me this much about her cousin's ceremony.

It was the doctor's clinic again, which were usually busy. Frances went to pick the doctor up at the dock and bring him up to the clinic. Right at the end of the clinic as the floatplane was landing at the dock, two very weary Calgary teenagers turned up at the clinic door. Frances took the doctor to the plane. The girls were with the YWCA from Calgary, Alberta and had been out on the ocean in the sun canoeing all day. They were dehydrated. We brought them into the clinic's only bed and positioned then feet to feet. I started a slow Intravenous infusion and hung both bags of fluid from the only pole we had. I darkened the room and let the girls sleep. Not long after that someone came into the clinic and told me that someone had been found dead in an old disused house. Rhea had gone home half way through the clinic with a migraine headache and Bruce was out of the community on vacation. I asked the person if they could take Colleen to the house as I had two people in the clinic and could not leave. I called Colleen and explained the situation to her and could she please investigate the situation then come up to the Clinic.

This done, Colleen came back and as the girls were stable, I asked Colleen to stay with the girls and I quickly went to the house where the body was found to ensured the person was dead and came back to the clinic. I called the RCMP to let them know and they said that they would notify the coroner.

Then I called Bella Bella to have the doctor confirm the death. In the Arctic, I can sign death and birth certificates, but in British Columbia a death certificate has to be signed by a Medical Doctor. Then I called Charlotte to let her know what was happening. The two girls from Calgary were now rehydrated and were able to rejoin their camping trip. They were very grateful and left us T-shirts from the YWCA. They would wear sun hats and drink lots of water when they next set foot in their canoes.

Next event was the funeral and the preparation for the young man's burial, which lasted a week. There was a church service every evening followed by a supper. On the last day the burial took place and only the few chosen from the community went off in a boat to the burial island. In the evening, there was a Potlatch, which we were all invited to attend and receive a gift according to our status in the funeral preparations. I received kitchen items in a basket.

My residence was in a trailer just up the hill from the clinic and I had some very friendly wolf like puppies and their mother for companions. I often went up to the top of the hill to get a wonderful view of the panorama.

One day, while I was up at the top of the hill, Murray came looking for me as some one was choking in their home. Bruce who lived near this person had gone over to see to things. Murray drove me to the house and all was well. Bruce, Marge, Rhea and I often went for walks around the harbour and looked at the fishing boats.

Kay, the Regional Nursing Officer, and Charlotte from the South Mainland Office came over to visit from Vancouver. I enjoyed showing these ladies around and Charlotte stayed over for a few days. It was time for me to move down to one of the Health Canada Houses. While I was making this move, I checked out one of the storage sheds beside the house. It was full of outdated medications. I would have to move these to the clinic and gradually transport them out with the doctor's charter to the hospital in Bella Bella for destruction. It is just as well that I found this deposit as we were already having problems with teenagers who wanted to sit in the house where the young man had committed suicide.

I had a meeting at the request of several elders who wanted this house barricaded and the police to keep a watch on the house. This was done and no more untowarded events occurred.

The school graduation was almost upon us and I went to the school to finalize the immunization program. The evening of the graduation was most entertaining and the graduates were all given beautiful hand made button blankets. We had another wonderful feast.

I would soon be leaving and Marianne made me two beautiful crocheted wall hangings that now are framed and hang above my bed. Sam Duncan brought me a painting of an owl, which is the sign of death. But as he explained the owl's feet are not pointing down on the roof; they are pointing out which is the sign of a healer.

It was time to leave Klemtu and go home for a short break. Then I would be working out of Victoria and traveling daily by ferry to the South Mainland Zone Office in Vancouver. I would be the Special Projects Nurse doing Suicide intervention with Tribal Councils in the lower main land, which would constitute more land traveling.

Chapter 23

༃

SOUTHERN BRITISH COLUMBIA

I N SEPTEMBER 1995, I was living at my home in Victoria and traveling Monday to Friday on the Ferry to Vancouver. On a Monday, Charlotte would meet me at the Ferry Terminal and we would sail together to Vancouver. The South Mainland Zone Office was where my office was located and this was near City hall in Vancouver. I worked closely with the psychologist and while he was on vacation, I would travel throughout the lower mainland to meet with the tribal councils on suicide issues.

In Delta, I had a meeting with the Tsawwassen Band. This progressive lower mainland group's territory was on the way to the Ferry terminal. The Tsawwassen Band is quite involved in commercial enterprises in the area and operates a golf course and a casino.

I traveled to Penticton, where I met with the Penticton Indian Band, who are members of the Okanagan Tribal Council and that was a very fruitful and pleasant meeting. After the meeting, I stayed in Penticton at the Lakeside hotel with a beautiful view of the Okanagan Lake, but unfortunately I did not see the Ogopogo, a creature similar to Nessie of Loch Ness in Scotland. Whether either of these creatures actually exists is a mystery.

Next day, I went to West Bank First Nations' Territory and following my meeting with the members, I had a lovely tour of Whispering Pines, a care center for the Elders. Then I drove to Creston and met with the Lower Kootenay First Nation and interestingly their linguistic affiliation is Kootenayan and this is where the name of Kootenay is derived from.

I spent the night in Creston and the following day I met with St.Mary's First Nation in Cranbrook, who share the same language affiliation as the Kootenay First Nation.

One day, I was on my way to Vancouver, on board the Spirit of Vancouver Island, when an announcement informed the passengers that two engines had failed and we were only sailing on the two other engines. I had to call the office in Vancouver and let them know that I would be at work as soon as I could. Well that was two hours later than I normally was in Vancouver.

The regional nursing conference was held in Harrison Hot Springs Hotel, which is located at the southern end of Harrison Lake and set against the spectacular snow-capped mountains of Southwestern British Columbia. Lush woodlands, soaring peaks, wildlife and waterways surround it. The hotel has a sulphur spring spa and it was a wonderful location for a mid-week meeting with co-workers. After our daily meetings we all took advantage of the soothing hot spring pools and the Copper Room restaurant that offered fine cuisine and an elegant ballroom for dancing the night away. I met some of my old acquaintances at the conference. Charlotte was the conference coordinator and fellow participants were Joanne from Dalhousie University and Margaret and Trish from Prince Albert in Saskatchewan.

After the conference, I had decided that I should stay in Victoria for a spell as I was becoming too much of a nomad. I would start work at Beverly Lodge in Victoria, which was a supported living facility. After a month or so there I joined a Human Rights support Organization called Building Bridges in Chiapas, Mexico. I thoroughly enjoyed our fund raising efforts in planning and operating dances with the Latin Band Kumbia, Art shows and doing the secretarial duties for the group. We did education seminars in the community and worked along with the Latin American Support Group at café Simpatico. Then in March 1996, the Red Cross asked me to go to Kyuquot. I was ready to wander again.

Chapter 24

ᡃ

KYUQUOT

I N SPRING 1996, I flew into Comox, British Columbia, taxied to Gold
River and boarded the float Plane for Kyuquot. Standing on the main
island dock was Janette whom I recognized from the Red Cross
outpost hospital in Alexis Creek. What a small world. The Red Cross
speedboat zipped down the channel towards Okime Island, my home for
the next few months. I would have to learn to operate the speedboat. Life
is a learning curve.

The remote region, Kyuquot Sound, lies south of the Brooks Peninsula
and north of Nootka Island on the West coast of Vancouver Island.
Accessible only by air and water, it is scattered with islands and rocky
shoals. Road access for the region is at Fair Harbour, where there is a government dock, an unsupervised campsite and room for parking. Kyuquot
is a charming little wilderness community on several islands with the occasional small logging camp. There are no cars and no alcohol. The coastal
steamer Uchuck 111, an old minesweeper, comes once a week from its port
in Gold River and brings heavy goods and dangerous good such as my
oxygen tanks for the Red Cross Outpost Hospital.

Kyuquot is the traditional territory of the Kyuquot/Checlesaht First
Nation amalgamating in 1962 retaining Kyuquot as the Band name with
26 reserves on 382 hectares they are members of the Nuu-chah-nulth
tribal council. Archaeological sites containing the remnants of cultures
that thrived here over the past several thousand years have been identi-
fied. The original village site is on Aktis Island, where more than 2,000

Natives lived pre contact European years now has only about 30 residents. Gooyducks are harvested from the rocks by First Nations people and sent to Japan, where there is a thriving market in this seafood delicacy.

Historically in European times, Kyuquot Sound once had thriving fur trading and whaling industries and as demand decreased and populations diminished, locals turned to fishing to make their living. Today there is still evidence of the remains of the Cachalot whaling station. Commercial fishing, and to a lesser extent logging, finfish and shellfish aquaculture, sport fishing and adventure tourism are now the region's primary economic activities.

Kyuquot has a school Kindergarten to grade 12, on reserve land, although many of the non-native children are home schooled. The mail is flown in and out three times per week to the post office, which is on the main island and doubles as a general store. Approximately 500 people both Native and non-Native people reside in Kyuquot. The Non Native houses have lovely vegetable gardens, and a boardwalk rims the bay. There is a resident sea otter that would swim out in front of the Red Cross outpost and munch on his sea urchins. He was fascinating to watch. The resident seal is named "Miss Charlie" and has lived there for 37 years. She even has a restaurant named after her (excellent food). I had no idea seals lived so long. Across the bay, on another island, is the First Nations community. Various other islands within a short distance have houses or shacks some big and some small, fancy or run down.

Janette has three sheltie dogs and two cats and a husband that would remain behind for a short while when Janette went out on vacation.

Janette's husband was a chef and made wonderful meals and fresh bread. He was the nephew of the multimillionaire, Jimmy Pattison from Vancouver, British Columbia.

Janette left the next day and a terrible storm was blowing. The thought of learning to operate a speedboat in that weather did not thrill me.

The telephone system was rather different in that one could call locally in the normal fashion but to make a long distance phone call one had to connect to the long distance operator in Vancouver.

It was time for my driving lesson in the speedboat. Janette's husband gave this and I only had one lesson. Then he left Kyuquot to join Janette on her holiday and medical leave. Well I had to get with it, as I had to leave my Island to visit patients, the school, the First Nations Community Health Representative and collect the mail. The currents at my dock were very strong and if the tide was turning the currents were even stronger. When I drove over to the reserve, the First Nations residents would come down to the dock to help me moor the boat and to preserve the dock. I gradually learned how to be a little gentler in my docking skills.

When I went to collect the mail, the fishermen would lean over their boats, and tease me calling out here comes the skull and cross bones not the Red Cross flag boat. Another day, while I was attempting to dock at my island, I got hung up on the rocks. The tide was turning and the engine was stuck on the rocks. I tried to push away, but to no avail and I thought that the boat should have a set of oars, but there weren't any to be found on board. Luckily, I had a radio, which was tuned into channel 16, the coast guard channel. My housekeeper, Joanne, lived on the next Island and I called her on the radio to come in. She was there and she came out in her boat and rescued me. Next task was to find the oars, which were in the boathouse and secure them on the boat.

One day, Joanne and Cindy, a friend of Joanne's, and I went off for a boat ride in Joanne's boat. We went to the island called Dead Man's island. It was called this as many years before the European settlers had arrived in Kyuquot; the Haida Nation had a battle with the Kyuquot and Checlesaht First Nations. The Haida Nation won and it was the custom not to bury the defeated, but leave the dead warriors on the ground naked. I did not see any bones lying around, but I did collect some amazing specimens of moon snail shells, which I have in my house decorating one of my bathrooms. The three moon snail shells sit in three-cedar hand woven basket made by an elder from Klemtu.

One of the home school children had measles and had never been immunized. To confirm my diagnosis, I had to do a serum level and the results would be part of a Mayo Clinic measles survey that was on going. The result did in fact confirm the diagnosis. Many children in third world countries, who are not immunized, die from this childhood disease.

There had been an earthquake just off the coast near the Queen Charlotte Island and the quake had registered 6 on the Richter scale. I called down to the emergency preparedness centre in Victoria and there was a tsunami-warning out. I called the reserve to make sure that the residents knew what to do. Our plan is to go up the hill to the school and we have our emergency supplies up there. That was great news, as I had no plans of traveling in my boat until the warning was over. I too would stay up on my hill.

I would from time to time call my answering machine at home in Victoria. To do this one had to go through the long distance operator. I could not get the message machine to play back my messages. So I asked one of my neighbours in Victoria to go into my house and check my messages for me and call me back from the house. It was a message from Margaret Mary asking me to call her in Aberdeen. I thanked my neighbour and called Margaret Mary. She told me that my mother had died and that the funeral had been announced the evening before the event and that she had not even been able to get there. That day she was at a court case in the High Court in Edinburgh. Uncle Marshall had gone with Anna and Harold and my sister had turned her back on Uncle Marshall and totally ignored him. I thanked Margaret for the information and told her that I would be home after my contract was over in Kyuquot.

The doctor from Sayward would fly into the reserve and then come over for a chat with me. He worked for the Nuu-chah-nulth tribal council and the non-Native population had a doctor who flew by helicopter into the Red Cross from Port McNeil. Neither doctor would turn away a patient because of the patient's origin.

One evening, a young baby came to the clinic. She had respiratory syncytial virus, RSV, which is the infection that I dreaded the most especially in very young children. The air way narrows very quickly and intensive care is adamant.

In the back of beyond this equipment is not available. The child requires a highly technical environment in a tertiary care hospital. I called for a medivac, but unfortunately the winds were too strong in Vancouver to permit the helicopter to fly to Kyuquot. I called down to speak with a pediatric physician in Children's hospital in Vancouver and was asked what the oxygen saturation level was. Unfortunately I do not have a metre I told the pediatrician. All I can do is give you the clinical exam details.

He was quite happy with my clinical report, but had I been working for the Arctic Governments, we had metres that read the oxygen saturation levels. The pediatrician agreed with me, even although this was probably a virus, we should give the baby intramuscular antibiotics in the event that a secondary bacterial infection was present. As soon as the winds died down, we would get the helicopter out to Kyuquot. The parents did not want to watch me give the baby the injection, but I assured them it was necessary and I would have to give it, as the baby was very sick. All night, I worked with the sick baby and around 10 am the helicopter and the pediatric medivac team arrived with an incubator. Off went the baby to the hospital with the mother. Another family had joined us just as the sick baby was about to leave. I assumed it was a relative and it was customary in the Native communities for everyone to come to the clinic, when a member of the community was sick. Once the helicopter took off, I found out that this was not a farewell party situation, but an attempted suicide. The young man had slit his wrists a few days ago. Now that the family was aware of this, they had brought the young fellow to see me. I treated the wounds and did some counselling and made an appointment to see him in a few days. It was time to get the mail. I was really very tired. I went down to the dock untie my boat. I had my reading glasses perched on top of my head and when I bent down my glasses fell into the water and was swept away in the current. Now what do I do? I cannot see to read the prescription labels or see to put stitches in. I would have to find a replacement or tell Red Cross that I was not safe to practice, as I could not see properly to do my work.

Off I went to the post office to get the mail and I asked if there were any glasses in the lost and found or if anyone in the store, at the time, had an old pair I could use. No one had any unused glasses. I went over to the reserve and the Community Health Representative, Rose, opened up the desk drawer and gave me a pair. I could read again. Then her phone rang. It was the school. A Teacher had been using scissors that had slipped and cut her hand. Tell her to come over to the clinic and I will take a look with my new glasses. I explained what had happened as I stitched her hand and we both laughed.

At the end of every month, I had to complete the accounts ledger. This was the job I hated most, as I could never get the accounts to balance even though I checked my entries everyday and thought that I had the books balanced. Nowhere else that I had ever worked was this part of my job and just as well, as I might never have lasted so long traveling in the isolated communities. The Red Cross charge, Non Native persons for the medications plus a pharmacy fee. There was also a fee for bandages and dressing material. The Native people were not billed but the billed amount was sent to the Federal Government to pay the Red Cross. I had to submit a narrative report as I had everywhere else and request all medications and equipment.

I asked for a hemoglobin meter and an oxygen saturation monitor both pieces of equipment were common place elsewhere that I had worked. I am pleased to say that when Janette came back to Kyuquot that both these pieces of equipment were on site.

One morning, I had a call from the Band office the chief wanted me to come and give a presentation on gas sniffing that afternoon at 2pm. I have people coming from other places to hear you. Well I said that I would do my best. We will meet in the big house. I had no literature at hand and no Internet or computer to find any and certainly no audiovisual material. There was no time to acquire this either. I would have to do this off the top of my head. Well there were about 600 people there and we all sat in a circle and exchanged information. The meeting went on for four hours and really it worked out as a positive experience. I used the examples of my experiences in Davis Inlet and the explosion in Cambridge Bay where the five teenagers were high on gas. They lit a cigarette and only three survived with severe burns and resulting in lasting facial scarring. The other two teenagers went up in smoke.

It was time for Janette to come in on the floatplane and I would meet her on the dock and exchange the narcotic keys and fly to Gold River.

Then back to Victoria and prepare for my trip to the United Kingdom. I would fly to London, where Wendy would meet me. Then Wendy, Gordon and I would drive to Aberdeen to attend 150th anniversary of St. Margaret's school for girls' reunion luncheon. The following day it would be 100th anniversary of Convent of Sacred Heart School reunion luncheon.

How fortunate to time both my two old school anniversary celebrations and catch up with my old school friends.

Chapter 25

ᛃ

TRIP TO UNITED KINGDOM AND VICTORIA, BRITISH COLUMBIA, HOME CARE

IN LATE June 1996 I arrived in London Wendy met me and Wendy Gordon and I drove to Aberdeen where Wendy and I attended St. Margaret's School 150th anniversary luncheon for former pupils. I started St. Margaret's School in the nursery class at age 3½. I recognized most of my old class. Three of the girls had started nursery at the same time as I had. At age 12, I had left St. Margaret's to join my cousin, Margaret Mary, at the Convent of the Sacred Heart where the following day, Margaret and I joined the old pupils and teaching nuns in the 100th anniversary celebration luncheon. All my old class was there. Strangely, the nuns were no longer dressed in their habits and I could not recognize any of the nuns. I sat at the lunch table next to a lady and asked where Mother Farley was? You are sitting next to her was the reply. We are all Sisters now as the Pope told us that we had to be on an equal footing with the non teaching Nuns. When I attended the Convent, the teaching nuns and the nun who was the doctor were called Mother and the remaining nuns who attended to the running of the houses were called Sister.

In August 1996 it was time for me to go back to Victoria and start a new job.

In September 1996, I was offered a job doing home care staffing. I was the after hours coordinator in this organization. At one point, I found this exceedingly challenging, when we had a tremendous snowfall in Victoria, which came to be known as the blizzard of 96. The severe winter weather in the concluding week of 1996 reached a crescendo in the 75-year record snowfall of December 28 and 29. The area affected included most of the southern third of British Columbia. During the day, the snow continued, once again setting a single day snowfall record for a city of 67.5 cm. on top of the snow already on the ground. Over the next 24 hours, winds would build drifts from the fresh powdery snow. Then rain and milder temperatures would add weight to the metre-deep (or deeper) snow, collapsing or damaging greenhouses, marinas, and buildings. As more rain fell, some areas experienced flooding and landslides. Even though the succession of weather events was accurately forecast, some people were "caught out" by the effect of compounding situations. Individuals, choosing to wait out routine activities such as grocery shopping and picking up medical prescriptions found that they could not wait to venture out for things deemed essential to them, and which they had not been able to get, in many cases, since before December 23rd. On December 23 there had been a significant snowfall then businesses were closed from December 25-26. Then the uncleared snow on December 27 and 28; and a new heavy snowfall on December 29; and lack of equipment to clear streets for some, escape, was not until January 2. Many people who thought that they were prepared to be patient for a couple of days, simply lost their patience and became angry with government response and any other target they could find to criticise. Old-timers expressed the opinion in local media that the 1916 storm was much worse than the now-called Blizzard of '96. Clearly, statistically, the Blizzard of '96 involved much more snow. If the current storm is not seen as being as significant an event, it is because we are able to respond better to snow conditions today, even if Greater Victoria is not prepared to deal with such storms as routine annual events. A single snowplow in the city's inventory of equipment was unable to cope. The city's fire department trucks and ambulances were stuck all over town. The military was called out to shovel the snow from the streets, mainly to allow emergency vehicles to operate, and in about eight days nature had allowed things to return to normal. The above accounts were published in the Victoria Times Colonist Newspaper throughout the Blizzard of '96. As the weather reports describe, Victoria came to a stand still and I had the arduous task of totally revamping all my staff bookings, which were normally done by seniority of the employee. This had to be changed to who lived nearest to a certain client and could the staff walk there. For an entire week I worked from 5.30 am until 1. 30 am reconstructing the administration of my staffing /client roster, which changed on a daily basis, and telephoning both staff and clients of the daily changes. There were times, when the elderly shut in clients that our home care agency served had no staff able to reach the client. I had to wrack my brains as to whether there was a building manager in the apartment block, or did one of my ex nursing colleges live anywhere near the client. Oddly enough I did achieve my staffing goals with thanks to all the staff and my friends.

A friend, June, from Inuvik in the Arctic was visiting her family in Victoria and I should have had some time for a rendezvous with June, but no such luck. We managed a brief telephone conversation and we totally agreed that the snowfall in 1996 in Victoria beat the Arctic records for the amounts of snow fall in one day.

In January 1997, a friend of mine, Birkby, called to tell me to apply for a job with Canada Pension Plan in the disability section. So I did and Birkby provided me with a reference. So in March 1997, I started work as an occupational health specialist with Canada Pension Plan in the downtown office in Victoria.

Chapter 26

ح

FORT MCPHERSON IN THE ARCTIC CALLING AND ON TO TURKEY

I WAS ENJOYING my administrative job in Victoria analyzing applications for disability pensions, which involved many changes to the Canada Pension Plan Legislation. This type of work had always been handled in Ottawa, but a decision by the Federal Government to regionalize this program to the provinces had started on a small scale and Victoria was one of the first places where the regional program would take place. There were only a few of us working in this situation and we had two people who had previously worked in the department in Ottawa, who had decided that they might like to relocate to Victoria, British Columbia. We worked in a multidisciplinary team structure. The team consisted of financial analysts in other programs of Canada Pension Plan, who were focused on different areas, unlike the disability specialists who had to focus on incapacity. For me this team structure made life more interesting, but that was not going to last for ever.

I spent time in my capacity of volunteer secretary of my human rights support group, Building Bridges in Chiapas, Mexico. We had monthly meetings and I met some very interesting people, who were of a similar mindset. Steve, who worked with the Human Rights Commission in Victoria: John, an artist. Tim was a Masters of English student at University of Victoria and worked with the developmentally challenged in the group homes. Alvaro from El Salvador with a degree in Agriculture and master's degree in Rural Sociology and Chris, a retired naval officer. Tim, Steve and I would run dances as fundraisers with the Latin Band Kumbia that Alvaro played in. These events were always fun, well-attended and great money raisers.

In January 1998, I received a phone call from the owner of a nursing agency in the interior of British Columbia. The owner, Charles, introduced himself and told me that he had worked in different places in the Arctic and Kyuquot, British Columbia and had noticed my documentation in the patients' charts. The call of the North was still in my blood. So when offered a job in Fort McPherson, I signed up for a 2 week contract to go to Fort McPherson during a holiday break from my desk job in Victoria.

Off I went on my two-week contract. I flew to Edmonton where I stayed in my old stomping grounds motel, the Nisku Inn. Then on to Inuvik and was met there by the (RCMP), Royal Canadian Mounted Police, who took me down to Fort McPherson, 121 kilometres south of Inuvik along the Dempster highway and 1107 northwest of Yellowknife. His wife was one of the Nurses at the clinic in Fort McPherson.

This community of 900 people is the home of the Teetl'it Gwich'in, "people of the head waters or people in the middle". The traditional name for the community is Teetl'it zheh, named after the Gwich'in name for the Peel River, Teetl'it njik. The languages spoken are Gwich'in, and English

In 1848 Fort McPherson was named after Murdoch McPherson who established a Hudson Bay post trading furs with the Gwich'in and Loucheux First Nations and Inuvialuit Inuit. In 1899 Fort McPherson played a role in providing supplies to the Yukon Gold Rush miners. Around the same time the Anglican mission moved to the area and in 1903 the RCMP built a detachment here.

I settled in and was ready for work. My first task on call was to be called out by the RCMP to identify a body that had been found in freezing temperatures frozen in the snow. The body was clad in a pair of underpants and a pair of socks. He had last been seen alive at approximately 3 am that morning. He was reported to have been drinking heavily. This information came from the policeman who was handling the paperwork. It was my job to determine the date and time of death. Now I had a date and an approximate time of death. As it is too expensive to send bodies from in the Arctic to Edmonton for autopsy, it is up to the community health nurse to investigate a sudden death and notify the coroner. My next task was to obtain body fluids from this frozen body. To attempt to put a needle into the vein or chest to obtain blood just caused the needle to bend. The last area of fluid in a body to dehydrate is the vitreous humor in the eyeball. I obtained some and sent it out to the laboratory in Yellowknife for analysis. I then called the coroner and on call physician at the hospital in Inuvik and explained the situation. Both agreed with the situation and we would wait for the report on the analysis of the vitreous humor. If nothing untoward was revealed then I would go ahead and sign the death certificate and the police could release the body from their mortuary for burial.

The next patient was brought in under police officer escort. He had been out hunting moose with his brother and the two men had brought home a moose. That afternoon the patient had consumed a bottle of rum and he and his brother had had a fight over who would keep the moose they had killed. In the anger that arose out of this altercation, the brother threw the patient out of the living room window. At the time, the patient was dressed in his underpants. The police had given the man a thick housecoat to wear. I attempted to assess his conscious level, but with all this alcohol on board it was rather a cloudy issue. He also required some stitches in his face. I closed the wound and then the policeman told the man that he would take him home. The man pleaded with the policeman to lock him up otherwise his brother would kill him. What ever happened to the Northern traditions of sharing the kill? While I was busy with this man, I received a call from a 96-year-old elder, who could not breath and was having chest pains. The lady had a long history of cardiac heart failure. I called my colleague as I could only deal with one patient at a time and the elder needed the ambulance and an escort to bring her to the clinic. The police offered to stay with the man, but that is against the Health Centre rules to leave the premises when one had an in-patient.

My colleague went to collect the patient and the man left with the policeman. Then I called the medivac and had to drive out in the dark to the airport to collect the medivac team. The pilot could switch his landing lights on from the plane. This was a far cry from when I first went north and had to call a crew out to light the runway, shovel the area and refuel the plane. The medivac crew landed and we went to the clinic, collected the elder and took her out to the airport for the flight to Yellowknife.

Life was not all work and it was time for the RCMP secretary's retirement function. I was not on call, so I could imbibe and enjoy the refreshments. We all spent a pleasant evening and later in the year I would meet the secretary's son in Victoria.

After we left the house, where the festivities were held, we stopped and whistled at the northern lights, which flashed across the sky in this freezing cold environment. Inuit legend said that the lights would whistle back.

Soon it would be time to go back to Victoria as two weeks go by very quickly.

Back to my office and plan to run a fund raising art show for Building Bridges. I was also planning a Christmas holiday in Turkey to explore the archeological sites.

In April 1998, I was invited to represent to Northern Nurses at the Commissioning of the HMCS Yellowknife in the Esquimalt naval base. My friend Chris was present representing the naval Cadets. It was a very cold day and we sat waiting for the ceremony to start at the Naval Dock yard in Esquimalt. The first speech was given by the Inuit representative in the Canadian Senate, similar to the House of Lords in UK.

This was Senator Willy Adams and he stood up at the podium and put his speech down. The wind blew it away and he said, "*I thought we only had wind like this in the Arctic and I did not expect this in Victoria.*" All the audience laughed as we were anticipating very formal speeches. How refreshing this was. After the ceremony, we all went to the marquee for refreshments. The navy does know how to cater. Chris told me that the evening dinner would be even more impressive and it certainly was. For those who knew the Arctic fare, the Dene and Inuit participants in the commissioning of the HMCS Yellowknife brought down Char, Moose and Musk ox from their homeland. After a wonderful feast, the next morning we would go for a sail on 706, HMCS Yellowknife.

I had been doing too much walking resulting in my injured foot collapsing again, but this was not going to stop me from exploring Turkey. In December 1998, I flew to Ankara loosing all my luggage en route leaving me to tour the noncommercial areas of Turkey in one beige outfit. I arrived in Ankara airport where approximately 40 Turkish young male taxi drivers swarmed towards me. I had my collapsible cane with me to help me walk pointing it to the very back of the crowd of taxi drivers. At the hotel, I joined my group and had an enjoyable meal. The next morning, we started our tour in Ankara visiting museums and archeological sites including Troy and Ephesus and concluding our tour in Istanbul where I was fascinated to watch whirling Dervish in a unique performace at our hotel. It was rather an interesting trip as we were celebrating Christmas and New Year and the Turkish community was celebrating Ramadan. Sad to say it was time to go back to work in Canada.

Chapter 27

ҁ

EMPLOYMENT EQUITY AND TEZIHUTLAN, PUEBLA, MEXICO DISASTER

W HEN I returned to my work in Victoria, the Director General, Steve Barnard appointed me to the Employment Equity Committee. This committee complemented my interests in multiculturalism and Human Rights. The committee worked closely with Human Resources in ensuring that the Federal Government hired sufficient numbers of Aboriginal persons, disabled persons, women and ethnic persons to meet the Government quotas. We would have educational meetings and run special events. We worked very closely with the Public Service Commission. I had a role working with Shawn Dheensaw, who was Employment Equity Coordinator for the Centre for Leadership in Employment Equity, Diversity and Rejuvenation. We had educational venues to educate colleagues on services available in Victoria and British Columbia when dealing with clients such as blind persons, hearing impaired, library service for persons unable to leave their home and "Handydart", services to assist handicapped persons to get around Victoria and British Columbia. We had multicultural celebrations with food from all kinds of ethnic backgrounds and we dressed up in clothes from our country of origin. For our efforts we were congratulated in a letter from the Director General, which read: "I want to recognize and thank all of you for your efforts as members of our Employment Equity Committee. Your ideas and efforts have paid off well in educating and encouraging our staff to participate in this important programme.

Challenges remain and I look forward to continued progress in the New Year. Thank you from Steve Barnard, Director General, Canada Pension Plan". I thoroughly enjoyed this work and we had another event, where my friend, Alvaro, came to talk to us from the Inter Cultural Association on Multicultural diversity. Members of the committee received an award on International Women's Day. The invitation read as follows: from the Victoria Interdepartmental Committee on Employment Equity and Diversity at the Center for Leadership in Employment Equity, Diversity and Rejuvenation of the Public Service Commission, in partnership with the Pacific Council of Senior Federal Officials, are hosting a luncheon to recognize all the nominees who are members of the Director General's Employment Equity Committees for their achievements. Region Congratulations, your working colleagues, after a selection process, have nominated you as "*A Woman Making a Difference in the Federal Public Service.*" We all enjoyed a lavish lunch at a prestigious restaurant in Victoria.

I volunteered my time in the first aid post at the intercultural associations folk fest, which was a music and dance event. I also belonged to the Kiwanis club and in the fall of 1999, my friend, Ricardo, and I went to assist in Mexico.

In the fall of 1999, torrential rains and an earth tremor caused a landslide to bury alive approximately, 50 complete families in the mud from the village of Tezihutlan, Puebla, a mountain city 175 kilometers east of Mexico City. In Victoria, Ricardo Rizo-Ruiz and Annette Wetherly had collected clothing and toys, some of which were donated by Cordova Bay Kiwanis member, Ron Webster, his wife Barbara and daughter, Denise.

In this region of Mexico, 53 communities were affected by this deluge and subsequent mud burial, which brought the death toll to 650 people in this vicinity. The walled village graveyard above the Tezihutlan village held the water from the torrential rains and eventually, the water and mud buried the village. Ricardo and I went to the devastated area, which was covered in mist and guarded by the army. We showed our Canadian identification to the soldier, who let us into the area. The smell of dead bodies that had been covered with lime was not a pleasant experience. Then we traveled to the near by refugee centre and helped distribute the donated items of clothing and toys. Thank you to all who helped make the Kiwanis Golden Rule a reality by helping to build back the lives of the villagers of Tezihutlan, Puebla. The survivors of Tezihutlan wish to thank you from the bottom of their hearts.

Back in Victoria, November 2 is the Mexican celebration of the Day of the Dead. In the Christian calendar, November 2 is the day of All Souls. In Mexico this Christian festival is combined with pre Christian beliefs and celebrated as the Day of the Dead, El Dia de Los Murtos. Altars are set up for adult as well as children. The altars are decorated with many things including photographs of the departed. Flowers, special food and in the case of children, toys adorn the altars. The intention is to invite the spirits of the departed to once again celebrate with their loved ones on earth. This is a happy fiesta. As much effort is put into the preparation of the altars as one would do when preparing to welcome a guest. Special bread is made, which is only made for this specific occasion. Music, singing and dancing surrounds the altars to further attract and welcome the departed souls. Ricardo and several other Mexican friends and I set up altars in Ross Bay Cemetery in Victoria at the invitation of the Cemetery Society.

Chapter 28

ぐ

MULTICULTURAL EXPERIENCES IN THE YEAR 2000 AND ONWARD

I
T WAS time to celebrate the new millennium and I was part of the year 2000 celebrations. Now I worked in a new area for the Canadian auditor general, Sheila Fraser in the quality assurance programme. It was part of my job to scrutinize the operations of the Canada Pension Plan and should I find errors have the party, who made the error, correct it.

Celebrations for the year 2000, down town Victoria were great fun and all the entertainers came though me to be directed to their assigned venues. I was enjoying life in Victoria. "Building Bridges" ran a dance for the celebrations and that was a great fundraiser.

In 2001, I went to Jalapa to attend a crash course in Spanish at the University of Jalapa, Veracruz, Mexico. I stayed with Ricardo's parents. They were most hospitable and I was well entertained by the family and friends. One day I was serenaded by Esteban's college band. The musicians were all dressed in 15th Century costume. The grandmother, El Tigre, was a source of inspiration and dedicated to the Catholic Church down the road. Manola, the nephew, attended a private college, where I went with the family to celebrate the Mexican Flag Day. The two family dogs lived on the roof, which is the custom in this part of the world. When, the director of the University presented me with my certificate, I recited the poem, Rosa Blanca, and handed her a white rose. Interestingly, Jalapeno chilies are canned in Jalapa in an old factory called La Jalapeña.

I thoroughly enjoyed exploring Jalapa or Xalapa, which is also known as the "Athens of Veracruz" because of the strong cultural influence of its three major universities and also for the wide variety of cultural events in the theater, museums, street art. Near City Hall and Parque Juárez is the Pinacota Diego Rivera Art Gallery, which houses the widest collection of Diego Rivera's paintings in Mexico. In folklore, the Spaniards believed that Xalapa was the birthplace and home of the Florecita, literally little flower, and the most beautiful woman in the world. Even today, some people continue to adhere to this belief, and some natives insist that it is not a legend. The Totonacas were the first people who established themselves around the Macuiltepetl, a five-peaked hill, which is now a park. During the 14th century, four cultures settled in the territory, which today is known as Xalapa. In 15th century Fifth Aztec Emperor Montezuma, invaded the territory founding the Aztec Empire, which terminated with the arrival of the Spanish conquistadores in 1519.

In September 2001, I had planned a trip to China and Singapore. The trip was almost cancelled due to the bombing of twin towers in New York, which occurred at the time I was about to leave Victoria. Vancouver airport was full of grounded planes as it is the major airport on the west coast of British Columbia. All the hotels were full with stranded passengers and aircrew. I manage to get to Vancouver by ferry and then stay with friends over night and leave from Vancouver airport for China the next day. During my time exploring China, I visited many ancient sites and museums in Beijing, Xian, and Chunking sailed on the Yangtze River observing the construction of the Dam and concluding my China adventure in Shanghai. In Singapore the climate and botanical gardens were most enjoyable topped by a visit to Raffles hotel. It was a very interesting trip and well worth all the hassle.

International Women's day celebrations for the Employment Equity Committee of the Federal Government were held at the Canadian Forces Base Esquimalt. The guest Speaker was, Iona V. Campagnolo, *Lieutenant Governor of British Columbia* who was born in Prince Rupert. We had a chat about the Mission Ships that sailed out of Prince Rupert. Iona V. Campagnolo had been baptized on the Columbia and I had sailed on the Thomas Crosby V, which she had also sailed on.

The call of the north came again when I went on a cruise to Alaska with my friend, Ruth, from Dalhousie University. I had never had a chance to go dog mushing. So I took a flight in a helicopter to the Iditarod dog team's camp on the Mendenhall Glacier in Juneau.

The urge to do more hands on health care was ever present.

In March 2003, I flew to Puerto Plata in the Dominican Republic to volunteer as a member of the optical team on the Caribbean Mercy, one of the Mercy Ship Fleet, whose non-political mission is to improve the health and living conditions of the world's less fortunate people. I lived on board the MV Caribbean Mercy as a crewmember and had a very tiny-shared cabin with no porthole. Monday to Friday the day started at 5:30 A.M. The night before, I would hang out my belongings on the rail outside the cabin so that I could sneak off and dress in the shower room at 5:30 A.M. This way I did not disturb my roommate who worked in reception in the afternoons. After dressing I headed for the coffee and e-mail connections, two decks up. Breakfast was 6:30 A.M and this I ate on the foreword deck watching black diesel fumes pouring from the power plant. Diesel fumes were a part of the air in Puerto Plata. 8 AM the bus arrived and we drove though the moped fill streets to the hill where the army fort was located. This is the location, which the Dominican Republic Government had assigned to us to deliver eye and dental care. At 9 AM we went out to the gate of the army fort to let in the people with appointment cards. If people did not turn up for their appointments, we would let in other people in the line up to make up the quota. Once inside the eye clinic we gave admission sheets. The next stage was to do visual acuity testing with the tumbling E chart. We had translators to help us, but I tried to be very independent and communicated in Spanish. Once the visual acuity was established, the patient went on to have a health history and then to see the optician. Following the optical exam, the patient was either referred to the dockside unit for surgery or to have the recommended eye prescription and glasses frames fitted.

We had over 2000 pairs of donated glasses and had to match the prescription in the logbook. As sunlight is very strong year round in the Dominican Republic, it is necessary to protect the eyes from the harmful rays of the sun. Much teaching was done on the subject and many pairs of sunglasses were distributed. Once the glasses were fitted, intra-ocular pressures were measured. At noon we stopped for lunch and then started up the whole process all over again. All in all we saw approximately 200 people per day. We left for dinner on board at 5 PM. During my time, in the Dominican Republic, I was fortunate to meet and witness an ophthalmologist, who performs conductive keratoplasty, which is a new ophthalmic procedure. This is used for people who wear glasses for reading and have otherwise healthy eyes. If keratoplasty is successful it will restore your visual capacity and you can discard the glasses. There is instant benefit from this procedure. It does not of course prevent aging.

The Haitian People in the Dominican Republic have fled their homeland for freedom. Most of the people live on the sugar cane plantations and are paid a pittance. They lack even the basic rudimentary needs such as beds, toilets or running water. The pay is poor and there are no schools for the children. Other teams of volunteers from the Caribbean Mercy ship built schools and churches for the poor and needy in Puerto Plata and surrounding areas. One school was constructed in a village called *Aguas Nigras*, Black Waters, which did not have a school and if children did not have a birth certificate they could not attend school. The eye team was not permitted to see any Haitian People.

There were Spanish classes Monday and Friday evenings. I had the opportunity to go back to my old job as nurse practitioner when the Dominican Republic Government gave us permission to go to the jail and do health care. At the jail I met the Canadian Consulate, who was visiting a Canadian woman, who had been in jail for 3 years and had never had a trial. Someone had planted drugs on her and she was caught at the airport. Most of the prisoners were in jail for political reasons and had never had a trial and had been in jail for 20 years. If your family does not bring you food one does not eat. The Canadian woman's mother has to pay someone in the community to feed her daughter.

On the weekend we would go to the beach, or waterfalls in the jungle or into town to get ice cream. Transportation was usually by an open backed cattle truck with seats. Across the bay from the Caribbean Mercy there was a fort left over from the days of the conquistadors. If you have watched the series, Horatio Hornblower, the fort looks just like the forts in that series. Then there was an interesting cable car that ran up to the top of the mountain.

On the last Thursday the optical and dental team presented a skit to the crew entitled Three Blind Rats. This was very appropriate as the rats had taken over the dental and eye clinics but we had learned to cope.

Some people were more interested in escaping from life aboard the Caribbean Mercy on the weekends and headed for the plastic tourist resorts such as the Playa Dorado or Golden Beach. I went there on the last morning to get some Amber and Larimar.

Amber is fossilized resins, formally tree sap and a product of time and pressure. Most valuable pieces contain fossils of insects. Amber is mined between Puerto Plata and Santiago. Larimar is a pectolite and is light blue. I bought a pair of earrings made with both gems and a fossilized insect.

On returning to my desk job in Victoria, I contacted Maurice, from Watson Lake and Dalhousie University who had been appointed acting Zone Director for Health Canada in Prince George, British Columbia with the intent of returning to the North again. I called him and he knew right away who I was and asked me to come back to work in the North for Health Canada. Next day, I received an application package by special delivery post and the following day, I received a call from the recruiting officer. The thought of working in the North again was too much of a pull and I sent in the application. It was 8 years since I had really work as a community health nurse in an isolated region. Then I received a telephone message from my old boss, Charlotte, at Health Canada's regional nursing office in Vancouver stating that it was a voice from the past and to call her for an interview.

Chapter 29

༄

BACK UP NORTH

IN NOVEMBER 2003, I requested an unpaid leave of absence from my Federal Government administrative job in Victoria, British Columbia, Canada. I went back to work in Northern British Columbia with Health Canada's First Nations and Inuit Health Branch, working in 7 communities for varying periods of time ranging from 2 to 8 weeks pending on staffing requirements.

First there was Boot Camp in Prince George to up grade my hands on skills and ten exams later, I was awarded a certificate of competency so that I could work as a nurse practitioner as I had eight years previously.

In early December 2003, I was then posted to the out post clinic as the Nurse in Charge to a First Nation's community called Kitkatla, an island community an hour by seaplane off the North Coast of British Columbia between Prince Rupert and the Queen Charlotte Islands. Pryia met me on the dock and gave me my orientation. She was leaving Kitkatla and kindly left me the groceries that she had in her freezer.

This is rural living!! No grocery store, an old Anglican Church with no organ, piano or heat. It was a dreik Christmas Service without even a carol. We had 72 power outages from November until January. Each time the power went off the water stopped flowing from the water treatment plant. This instigated water to be shipped in to Kitkatla via barge from Prince Rupert. This tiny coastal island of 500 Tsishaman people had not seen snow for over twenty years adding to the challenge of the ever changing winds and no planes requiring one to stock up on food when the planes were flying. So if a very sick person had to be sent to the hospital in Prince Rupert you would pray that the weather would let the plane fly. If not, one had to look after the person with the whole village watching you until the weather permitted evacuation. While I was in Kitkatla, I took part in planning for 2004 Maternal Child Health manual. I was a midwife who had trained under the world-renowned midwife, Margaret F. Miles who wrote the Textbook for Midwives. I would be away on holiday in the Galapagos Islands when the conference was held in Vancouver. The Regional Nursing Consultant was Charlotte who has two masters' degrees in Nursing. I was given special mention for reminding us of the need for basics.

Early February 2004 it was time to leave Kitkatla and I flew to Prince Rupert where Lori was waiting for me on the seaplane dock. We sped off in a taxi to the Crest hotel where Lori and Kris were staying prior to going to Kitkatla. Enroute, I had to stop at a cash machine to get some money. Over a welcome glass of wine, I passed on the narcotic keys to Kris and gave my two colleagues the community report and caught my plane to Victoria

In Victoria I picked up my things and was off to Peru, Ecuador and the Galapagos. Victoria, British Columbia is over run by broom, in fact we have broom bashes. When I landed in Peru en route from the airport to the hotel, I thought that I was seeing things. I asked the guide was that broom? Oh yes and even in the high Andes there it was a- flowering and a-blooming. Fortunately it had not invaded the Galapagos Islands. One has a thorough inspection of all luggage and clothing to make sure you are not endangering these very unique islands and an entrance fee of $ 100.00 US and restricted numbers of visitors per annum.

The Galapagos was my favorite spot. I swam with a turtle, white tipped sharks and playful sea lions. We walked through colonies of masked boobies; blue-footed boobies and the male, magnificent frigate birds were all puffed up with red-ballooned chests to attract the females to the nest. The marine iguanas slept on the rocks warming themselves in the sun. The male land iguanas sat under the cactus tree guarding it from other males and attracting females by throwing down succulent flower and buds. These islands have no water and the plants are the only source of water until the rains come.

In March 2004 on returning from Galapagos, Klemtu was the next First Nation community with approximately 500 Kitasoo people. I had my personal tour of the new ceremonial house built where the white spirit bear came to the area.

This was my third visit to Klemtu across the straight from Bella Bella. During my time there we had a funeral. This celebration lasts for a week and each evening there is a United Church service followed by a feast. The feasts consist of wonderful seafood. Herring eggs with seaweed, halibut, sockeye salmon, clams and oolican oil are all part of the fare. The burial takes place in the afternoon before the feast and only the closest relative go in a boat to the island for this part of the funeral. The final evening is the settlement feast. I was presented with a donation to the clinic as a thank you for the clinic staff's part in the life of the deceased and the family.

In April I went on a two- week assignment to an inland area, Anihiem Lake, near Bella Coola where Sir Alexander Mackenzie once carved his name on a rock. There the community was larger and so was the consumption of alcohol, which increases the amount of accidents and generally poorer health and lifestyles. The Chilcoltin tribes live in this area and it is ranching country.

One of my Dalhousie University colleagues works in another out post further down highway twenty, a sandy dirty road. We met for dinner one night and I think that Ruth was so *bushed* that she ordered a steer instead of a steak. I remarked to Ruth that the cook did not have the steak tethered at the kitchen back door. We had a good laugh about that. I would be meeting up with Ruth again in 2005 in Tatla Lake.

In late April my next community was Telegraph Creek, Canada's best-kept secret. It was one of the places where gold miners went in the 1800's gold rush. Some of the Chinese miners names remain amongst First Nations surnames. These names are Quock, Han Yu and Quash. The stone walls and houses built by the Chinese miners still stand today without one inch of cement to hold them together. I must say I have never seen such an abundance of Western Swallow Tailed Butterflies. The community believes that when these butterflies are plentiful so is the supply of salmon. I watched the male Western Swallow Tailed Butterflies collecting minerals from the mud for dowries. The dowries are given to the female Western Swallow Tailed Butterfly before mating takes place. First Nations catch the spring Salmon in nets strewn across the river. I watched Sheila, the Community Health Representative, and her husband catch one of the 30-pound Spring Salmon in the Stikine River. Sheila took me for a tour of the fish camps where we watched community members who were canning and smoking the salmon. My colleague, Nancy, was the chief's sister also took me round the community. One day we went to the school sports where we watched a different version of the egg and spoon race. This was called the egg toss and two opposing teams throw raw eggs at one another. I enjoyed working in this traditional community. This is the land of the Talhtan Nation and I was adopted into the Crow Clan.

In late June I was assigned to Port Simpson located off the North Coast of British Columbia near the Alaskan border for a few more weeks of adventure. The weather was unreasonably hot and too much of a change for some of the elderly natives who are used to lots of rain. The older people had a hard time breathing in the dry hot air, which lacked the usual humidity. People were even watering the road to keep the dust down. There was a wolf came wandering into the village one day and this was very unusual. It was very thin and took off to Ross Island within a short space of time. It was nice to see the Port Simpson United Church that I visit in while I was on board the Thomas Crosby V. I had a very interesting meeting with the elders who explained what it was like to be a midwife in the old days and how the community had a cannery at the mouth of the Skeena River, which was called the Aberdeen. This of course reminded me of my hometown port of Aberdeen in Scotland.

In mid July my final posting was for 3 weeks to Fort Ware and Tsaky

Dene two very isolated communities north of Prince George and Mackenzie. Twenty years ago the government had made a hydro dam in this area to supply many areas with electricity including California. In turn for flooding the Native peoples' land the Government supplied new houses. The Native people put their dead in the ground, but cover the top of the earth with a spirit house. I must admit the graveyard looks unique. Now I am back in Victoria and preparing for my next adventure in Guatemala with Medicos En Accion in the early part of 2005.

Chapter 30

༄

GUATEMALA

IN JANUARY 2005, I trudged off with Medicos En Accion, a group of Physicians and Nurses from Canada for a two-week voluntary assignment in the highlands of Guatemala. We flew from Vancouver to Guatemala City then drove to Panajachel on the edge of Lake Atitlan.

This area is a world-renowned sight and is part of the ring of fire. Volcanic activity began in the Lake Atitlan area about 11-12 million years ago with a large explosive eruption occurring about 84,000 years ago forming the most recent caldera occupied by Lake Atitlan. On the banks of Lake Atitilan are three volcanoes San Pedro, Toliman and Atitlan.

We stayed at Hotel dos Mundos, two worlds, and one can see why. There are the Mayan people and the mostly American Gringos. The latter appear to be left over hippies from the sixties and are Marijuana happy.

In the morning we packed our gear and headed for the lake where we boarded a boat and set off on a journey across to the opposite shore of the lake towards San Pablo, a small village, up in the mountains with no form of health care. The language was one of the 30 plus Mayan dialects and we had to find a translator who could speak both Spanish and the native language. We saw men who were celebrating the feast of San Pablo dancing and wearing traditional masks and trousers.

After our day at the Mayan villages across the lake we would come down to the lakeside café and over an evening aperitif admire the lake and watch all the activities of the fishermen readying their nets for fishing early next morning.

We held a clinic in Chuchucu Village and we visited many villages with similar health problems lacking clean water. Despite the amount of water in the lake, water in the high mountain villages is in short supply and full of parasites and the source of many health problems. The Mayan people farm on the steep hillsides some times tied to a tree so they will not fall off the mountainside. The people are gentle and loving but only exist on a subsistence type of farming.

One-week end I took a trip to visit the local area with a tour guide and a driver. No one else in the group was interested in this activity so to the horror of all the Canadians, I went by my self. I had a wonderful day visiting and exploring the countryside. We visited the ancient pyramids, which were in the original Mayan Society and named in the book the "Popol Vuh", which is about the Mayan legends and beliefs. There was a pilgrimage passing as we traversed the pyramid site and my guide explained in detail what the people would be doing with the sacrifice of dozens of eggs that the people were carrying. We stopped at the sulphur hot springs of Fuetas Georgina, which were under repair. One could smell the sulphur from miles away. I was so well treated by these young men that I felt like I was their mother. This is the Latin culture. In Quetzaltenango, we met a local midwife who really would like a safer water supply. Photographs were not permitted when we visited a temporary shrine of San Simeon, the Maya people's chief saint, a mixture of the devil surrounded by alcohol and cigars and the appearance of a Spanish conquistador. He is greatly feared by all and money is pinned to him to keep the people safe. Much secrecy surround the exact location of San Simeon and his shrine is moved frequently from house to house. The Mayan people have kept their own calendar and religious beliefs despite the invasion by the Spanish conquistadors in the 1500s who attempted to convert the Mayan people to Catholicism. On the surface it appears that conversions had been accomplished as the feast days of the saints coincide with the Mayan ceremonies. One sees the Mayan people praying in church before a crucifix only to find out that they believe that Christ on the Cross is a blood sacrifice. In the same village the most beautifully decorated exterior Mayan Church had a duplicate at the opposite end of the street, on top of the steep hill.

Our two weeks in the Mayan culture was almost over and we would spend the last weekend in Antigua at the Hotel Quintas Flores where the surgical team of Medicos en Aciones was staying. Surgery was performed at the Hermano Pedro hospital built in 1680 in Antigua. The surgical referrals were from our isolated communities and it had been part of my recording duties to ensure that the referrals reached Antigua.

Time to fly back to Victoria and then off to let Ruth escape from Tatla Lake in the West Chilcotins. I had retired from my Federal Government job and I would now be working on contract for British Columbia Interior Health Authority in their only outpost station. When I worked there 14 years ago, the clinic was under the Federal Government jurisdiction.

Chapter 31

༄

RETIREMENT IN TATLA LAKE, WEST CHILCOTINS, BRITISH COLUMBIA

I
N EARLY February 2005, I flew over the coastal mountains on my way to Tatla Lake, British Columbia, where I had worked approximately 14 years ago so I knew the First Nation and the Non First Nation Community fairly well. I went to help Ruth, a Dalhousie University colleague in the backwoods of Tatla Lake who had to go to Vancouver with Teddy, her husband, who was to have cardiac surgery.

Before Ruth left in mid February to take Teddy for his surgery in Vancouver, the Community had the sporting events on Martin Lake. This was fun and it was good to get out in the fresh air. Some caribou came to feed on the lake, which was unusual as this was not the caribou's usual territory. We all enjoyed a weenie roast and hot chili with lots of home made cakes and cookies. Hot drinks were also plentiful to keep us warm.

At Martin Lake, I reacquainted myself with Helen and Ed, who were pioneer farmers and had been born in the area. I had a lovely visit with the pair who I had known when I was first in the area in the early nineties. I met many people from my previous experiences here. This included Iyla Charleyboy and her brother in law, Irvine Charleyboy, the Chief. Irvine wanted to know where I had been for the last fourteen years. My answer was "I have been wandering just like you".

Across the road from the clinic was Tatla Lake covered in ice and snow. Just further down the road was the Graham Inn, which was a pioneer family's home in the early 1900's. The Graham Inn was now under new management and it felt a little strange not to see Bruno there, but it still served an enjoyable meal and was a good community-gathering place. It was a pretty quiet community where one could enjoy the wonderful nature in the area and the various community events that took place. This was a ranching area and time for calves to be born and trumpeter swans to come back after wintering in warmer regions. The trumpeter swans nested beside the lake and made plenty of noise.

I worked with Janet, the secretary, three days a week who had a homestead next to the clinic and when she went to Williams Lake, she brought groceries back for me. Blood work was done once a week and taken to Williams Lake by B Line Courier.

I had a call from a young man who had suspected appendicitis. He had to make the three-hour ambulance ride to Williams Lake hospital for surgery. The end result was satisfactory.

Once a week, I would go home visiting to see Johnny, a 98-year-old retired rancher living by himself in a small house in the Tatlayoko valley. It was a lovely peaceful drive through the ranching country and past the famous Bubble Tree, which is shaped like a bubble by the winds in the area.

One day a truck driver dropped by the clinic with an injured Great Grey Owl that he had found on the road. It was a beautiful rare creature that sat on my clinic bench calling and turning its head in all directions. Janet went to get a cage from her home. The owl was my favourite patient and he had attempted to fly around the clinic room. I really do not know very much about animal care and we knew that the Great Grey Owl would receive the best care in the nearest raptor centre in Williams Lake. We told the truck driver where the rapture centre was in Williams Lake so that the man could drop the owl off on his way back there.

One day I received a call from the Registered Nurses Association in British Columbia appointing me to the committee that marks the Canadian Nurses Registration Exams in Ottawa for the Canadian Nurses Association. I would go to my first meeting in Ottawa in July. In June, I would meet in Vancouver with the Registered Nurses Association in British Columbia. Then I had a call from Alvaro from the Intercultural Association in Victoria asking me to use my wisdom to mentor international Nurses who were trying to get established in their profession in Canada. I thought that I was retiring from nursing?

The next call I received was from my old boss's secretary inviting me to a luncheon in Victoria so that I could receive my official thank you from Paul Martin, the Prime Minister. I had to respond that this would have to wait until May as I was working alone in the West Chilcotins until then and could not leave my post.

End of April 2005, I am flying back over the coastal mountains to Victoria.

Chapter 32

ॎ

VICTORIA AND OTTAWA

I N THE Summer I volunteered at the Royal British Columbia Museum in historical and natural history areas. It is very enjoyable meeting people from all over the world and relating the various pieces of information associated with the different venues.

In May I received my retirement good wishes and thank you from the Prime Minister.

In May we hosted at the University of Victoria the gathering of Choirs across Canada. This was a fun event with very serious music.

In June, I went to Vancouver and met with the review committee for the Canadian Nurses Association. We had to make sure that the questions were clinically correct. The chair of the committee was Isobel who had been my professor of community health nursing at University of Victoria. Isobel told me that she had included my recommendations in the new Nurse Practitioner programme at the University of Victoria.

In July, I traveled to Ottawa, to mark the Canadian Nurses' exam papers. Time was scarce but I was able to include visits to several museums and Parliament Hill. The visit to The Hill included the light show, the Changing of the Guard and a trip to the East Wing where I met Sir John A. MacDonald, a Scot, and Canada's first Prime Minister. Needless to say he was an actor. 2005 was a celebration year for the War Veterans of Canada. The Peace Tower is a memorial to the war veterans where there is a book of remembrance and the pages are turned daily.

Now I am helping mentor international nurses to become Registered

Nurses in British Columbia. We have a great shortage of Registered Nurses in Canada as there is in the rest of the world.

September and it was time to start up choir practice again and perform *The Last Night at The Proms*. Training programs were on going at the Royal British Columbia Museum and Climate Change exhibits were a challenge to explain to the visitors.

I would make my final visit to the snow in Antarctica and South America at the end of 2005. As the climate warms one has to adapt to the changes.

Chapter 33

ɕ

SOUTH AMERICA AND ANTARCTICA

O N DECEMBER 21, 2005, I left Victoria British Columbia, Canada
for Rio de Janeiro, Brazil, where I boarded MS Rotterdam.
The following day during a tour of Rio de Janeiro I discovered that Brazil is manufacturing ethanol from the stems and leaves of sugar cane and uses this in place of gasoline. I took a cable car ride to the top of Corcovado Mountain where the statue of El Cristo over looks Maracanã Soccer Stadium, Ipanema beaches, the Copapabana Palace and Sugar Loaf Mountain. Cocktails were served on deck in the evening sunset as we set sail for Uruguay. After the sumptuous dinner I watched the Brazilian Samba show in the theatre. The next morning we arrived in Montevideo Uruguay, which is one of the smallest countries in South America. Montevideo received its name, when the Portuguese explorer first laid eyes on the 435-foot tall hill at the mouth of the harbour and uttered *Monte vide eu* (I see a hill). Montevideo is built along the eastern bank of El Rio Plata. The water front avenue links the old city with the eastern suburbs. We explored the many sights of Montevideo including fabulous beaches, Batille y Ordónez Park, Padro Park and the Carrasco residential area once the site of a notorious jail, the plaza indepencia where El Teatro Solis is situated and is modeled after the opera house in Milan. We saw the monument to the Graf Spey, a pocket battleship that the German admiralty ordered to be sunk in December 1939 after a battle with the British fleet, and prevent its capture. Then on to the Palicio Legislavato considered the most beautiful Parliament build-

ing in the World. Inside this edifice there are 50 different types of marble. The Spanish colonial, Portuguese and Italian influence was evident in the many buildings we saw. On to a tour of Colón residential area we reached the Santa Rosa winery area where we toured the wine making process spurred on by wine and champagne tasting. Following this we were entertained to lunch and a Uruguayan culture show with folkloric dancing and singing including the Tango and candombe dances.

Over night we sailed down the Rio Plata to Buenos Aires, Argentina where we met up with my friend Gena who is teaching English there. A taxi was waiting to take us to the main sights. Buenos Aires has 39 barrios or districts. Buenos Aires is known as the Paris of the South. After a refreshing coffee in the Britannia bar, a reminder of the British Empire, we were ready to explore again. In the Barrio of San Templo on Calle Defensa and Parque Lezama is the Russian Orthodox Church, which is my favorite place in the "City of Warm Winds." Argentina is very much a ranching country with gauchos roaming the pampas so we had to have Lunch at a typical steak restaurant and sampled dulce de leche. Another reminder of the British Empire is the imprint of cannon balls that were fired by the British at the tower of Santo Domingo, a convent church dedicated to Our lady of the Rosary during the war of independence in 1806. In the church graveyard marble angels guard the mausoleum of General Manuel Belgarno a hero of the war of independence. Needless to say Gena and I had much to catch up on a personal note and we had a leisurely refresco in a swanky café over looking the fashionable shopping area on the Avenida Corrientes, a pedestrian only area packed with people. Back to the ship in time for a pre dinner tango show put on by the Argentinean world champions.

Over night we sailed past Punta del Este where we left the Argentinean river pilot and now we are en route to the Falkland Islands. The landscape looks like bleak sheep country and is very like some of the Scottish moorlands. It is hard to understand why Argentina and Britain fought over this area in 1982. Never the less the sheep are happy. The Falklands consists of two islands. On the West Island is Darwin and on the East Island, Port Stanley, which has small airport. Definitely, this is sheep country where tussock grass and low vegetation abounds the landscape and many rookeries cling to the cliffs. Rock Hopper Penguins and Albatross make their homes here.

Lots of entertainment on board made up for the now cooling weather.

We had guest lectures Tony Sopper, an ornithologist and two renowned geologists Paul Dalrymple, a specialist in micrometeorology who has worked extensively in this area of Antarctica and is managing editor of Antarctica Society Newsletter. A glacier and a mountain in Antarctica are named after him. Paul's doctorial thesis was on the Physical Climatology of South Polar Plateau. John Splettstoesser was the younger of the two geologists. He has extensive experience in Antarctica and is advisor to the International Association of Antarctica tour operators. He is the recipient of two Polar medals from USA and USSR for his work in Antarctica and is currently president of the American Polar Society. Then there was retired Captain Toomey from the Canadian Coast guard, an expert on the icebreakers. He would sail us through the icebergs in Antarctica. In preparation for the ice we had the movie "March of the Penguins". New Years Eve rolled around and so did the sea fog. The Rotterdam's log indicated that we are now at the South Shetland Islands the most northerly point of the Antarctica Peninsula. Elephant Island was enshrouded in the mist with zero visibility. In 1903, Elephant Island received its name when 22 members of Shackleton's crew were stranded there for 135 days and survived on the Elephant Seals and living under upturned boats. We could see nothing, but fog from our roost in the crow's nest base camp. Sailing on between Elephant Island and Clarence Island, we sailed south through the night to Hope Bay in the Trinity Peninsula. Hope Bay is named after three members of a Swedish expedition who spent a desolate winter in 1903 subsisting on seal meat. A stone hut still remains there along with other historic relic as a reminder of the heroic efforts of the explorers of this remote, harsh and beautiful land. Permission for cruise ships to visit Antarctica requires Government approval and it is possible for this to be removed at any time.

Six of the world's 18 species of Penguin can be found in Antarctica, which hosts an estimated population of 17- 20 million breeding pairs. Although Penguins are unable to fly and are very awkward on land, these birds are excellent swimmers and look like miniature dolphin swimming along side the ship. 0600 hours. Happy 2006 and there is rain and drizzle. We arrived in Antarctic sound through the South West entrance. At 0920 we entered the Weddell Sea at Rosamel Island.

1200 we passed Esparanza Research Station. In 1951, Esparanza Research Station was built here. Esperanza is Spanish for hope or expectancy. This is Argentina's territory. This is where the first child, a boy, was born in

1987 Antarctica's first citizen. There is a chapel, post office, infirmary and even a grave yard and of course Adélie penguins. 1900 hours Baily Head, Deception Island where there is an old volcano and smaller ships can enter the flooded crater. Here we spotted 5-6 Humpback whales and one collided with the ship just brushing it. Today we were awarded our Antarctica exploration certificate, which informed us that we were sharing in the footsteps of Roland Amundsen, Sir James Shackleton and Robert Falcon. Not quite the trip of *the Endurance* in January 1915 by Tomas Orde-Lees and Sir James Shackleton. Antarctica's huge ice sheet covers nearly 99% of its surface and accounts for 90% of the world's ice and holds an amazing 70% of all fresh water on earth. If this ice sheet melted, the world's oceans would rise precipitously. The ice cover of Antarctica is continuously moving. Large icebergs are formed at the edge of the mammoth ice shelves and glaciers cave off into the sea. Permanent floating ice shelves extend over vast areas; the largest of theses formations, the Ross Ice Shelf is the size of the American State of Texas. At night the Rotterdame had to dump two days of used shower or gray water and now we reentered Antarctic sound at Hope Bay.

January 2, 2006 Antarctica Rotterdam's Log

At 0600 hours we entered the Dallmann Channel. At 0800 hours the Gerlache Strait from Schollaert Channel.

At 0845 Errera channel and Cuverville Island where there is a mountain named after Paul Dalrymple and a ship the *Pangino* from Ushuaia.

1015 hours cruising in Andvoort Bay and Neko harbour.

1200-1215 hours the water boat passage to Paradise Bay.

Passed the Chilean Gonzalez Videla Station.

1305 Almirante Brown Station.

1505 Nuemayer Channel South bound.

1705 Port Lockroy Sawtooth Mountain range.

Off shore overnight in Bismark Channel and made more water which was a process that took place every 72 hours.

On January 3, 2006 0820 hours Scientific Staff come on board from United States Nathaniel Palmer Station. Palmer Station was built in 1968. The station can accommodate 44 people. It is only usually fully staffed during the summer months. Research focuses on monitoring marine ecosystems, atmospheric studies and the effects of increased ultraviolet radiation on marine and terrestrial communities. The ever-increasing ozone hole has prompted much of the interest in the latter. Climate change induced changes in sea ice conditions and snowfall has resulted in the reduction of the population of Adélie Penguins to fewer than 3300 pairs, down t by 60 % from 1974 and it has been predicted that they will be gone from the island altogether by 2014. At 0950 hours we reached North entrance to Lemaire Channel, which is situated between the Antarctica Peninsula and the Booth Mountain Range and has dramatically steep sides. It was discovered in 1873 by a German sealing expedition but was not navigated until almost two decades later. Named by Adrien de Gerlache and honours Charles Lemaire who explored the Congo. A rugged island off the Graham Coast of the Antarctica Peninsula is Kodak Gap and ice often blocks the passage. At 1100 hours we had to turn back due to ice at Loubat point. Furthest South Latitude 65.04. 1496 miles from South Pole, 86 nautical miles to the Antarctic Circle. 1400 hours disembark scientists from Palmer Station.

Information from the Rotterdam's Log On Wednesday January 4, 2006 At 1200 hours position 58 degrees 22.85 S 066 degrees 43.8 W. There was a fresh breeze, moderate seas and fog.

At 2140 hours we were in Passage to Cape Horn. In 1615 the Dutch navigator, Willem Cornelis Schouten, named the Horn, Hoorn, after his birthplace. Cape Horn is the most southerly point of South America and has a rocky terrain that rises to a height of 424 metres. Frequent storms, strong currents and icebergs make the passage hazardous at times. Rounding Cape Horn is an experience well known to mariners. After passing Cape Horn we sailed into the Pacific Ocean, reversed and head for the Atlantic Ocean and set sail for Ushuaia, Argentina.

0600 hours Thursday January 5, 2006 Ushuaia, Argentina, Terra del Fuego the land of fire so named when Magellan's crew first sighted this land, the native Indian population had fires burning everywhere to keep warm. Another name given to this region is Fin del Mundo, the end of the earth. Once a penal colony it is now a great wildlife tourist attraction. I spent a delightful time touring the Beagle Channel and saw three types of Fugus, southern beech trees, two evergreens and one deciduous, black bush, prickly heath, blue-eyed cormorants, skuas and sea lions. I visited the end of the world post office. We saw rheas feeding in the pampas and these birds resembled the Emu of Australia.

Leaving Ushuaia we sail up the Beagle Channel named after the ship that Charles Darwin sailed in. We sailed past the fascinating sights of The Romanche or Martial glacier. In Punta Arenas Chile we had a fascinating trip to Magellanic Penguin Colony.

We stood on deck in awe at the sight of the Amalia Glacier; the blue colouration in the ice depicts ice more than two years old. Then we had a talk on board the Rotterdam by geologists Paul Dalrymple and John Splettstoesser, the Grandeur Of the Glaciers. Glaciers are large, usually moving masses of ice formed in high mountains or in high latitudes where snowfall exceeds the melting rate of snow. Glaciers can be divided into four types alpine, piedmont, icecap, and continental. Alpine glaciers are found in high mountain ranges throughout the world, even in the tropics. When a number of alpine glaciers flow together in the valley at the foot of a range of mountains, they form extensive glacier sheets known as piedmont glaciers. Icecap glaciers are somewhere between an alpine glacier and a continental glacier. A perfect example is the glacier system that covers a portion of Norwegian Island group of Svalbard in the Arctic Ocean. The center of each Island is covered with an ice sheet that overlies a high plateau. At the edge of the plateau the sheet breaks into a series of Alpine glaciers that move down steep valleys, sometimes reaching the sea.

A continental glacier is a huge glacier blanket such as the one that covers almost the entire extent of Greenland, flowing outward from the northern and southern parts of the island. Because of its thickness, 2700 Metres, it rises high above the valleys and hills of the land beneath it. Near the seacoast the glaciers break into tongues of ice and when they reach the sea break off forming icebergs. A glacier of a similar type covers the whole of the Antarctic continent and has an area of about 13 million square kilometers. The volcanic majestic Andes Mountains hem Eastern Chile marking a fault in the earth's crust. Historically, earthquakes have devastated Santiago and Valparaiso.

In 1700s Alexander Falkirk was shipwrecked on the Juan Fernandez circa Valparaiso and this gave Daniel Defoe the idea for *Robinson Crusoe*.

In Puerto Montt, Chile is Lago Llanquihue, which is the second largest lake in Chile. The snow-covered volcanoes of Osorono and Calbuco are mirrored in the clear waters of the Lake. As the planet earth gets closer to the sun, the climate warms. This melts the snow and ice making it harder to get stuck in the snow and I must adapt to a warming climate.